"You don't feel like a bride?"

Jago sat on the edge of the bed. "But you should, Ashley. It's supposed to be a once-in-a-lifetime sensation."

"Not necessarily," Ashley returned sharply. "When the company's problems have been settled, I intend to make a life for myself. It might include marriage."

"You're already married, sweetheart— to me," Jago said smoothly, but there was a note in his voice that warned her to tread carefully.

"Well," she said lamely, "there's no real reason for us to feel tied in any way." The bedroom walls seemed to be closing in on her, making her acutely aware of his physical nearness. "Jago, please go. God knows, you've got what you wanted...."

"How do you know what I want?" His voice was somber. "That's something I could never make you understand, but it hasn't stopped me wanting to try!"

SARA CRAVEN probably had the ideal upbringing for a budding writer. She grew up by the seaside in a house crammed with books, with a box of old clothes to dress up in and a swing outside in a walled garden. She produced the opening of her first book at age five and is eternally grateful to her mother for having kept a straight face. Now she has more than twenty-five novels to her credit. The author is married and has two children.

Books by Sara Craven

HARLEQUIN PRESENTS
411—MOON OF APHRODITE
440—SUMMER OF THE RAVEN
459—WITCHING HOUR
487—DARK SUMMER DAWN
551—UNGUARDED MOMENT
561—COUNTERFEIT BRIDE
599—SUP WITH THE DEVIL
616—PAGAN ADVERSARY
647—A BAD ENEMY
704—DARK PARADISE
815—ALIEN VENGEANCE
832—ACT OF BETRAYAL
856—PROMISE OF THE UNICORN
872—ESCAPE ME NEVER
920—A HIGH PRICE TO PAY

SARA CRAVEN

the marriage deal

Harlequin Books

TORONTO • NEW YORK • LONDON
AMSTERDAM • PARIS • SYDNEY • HAMBURG
STOCKHOLM • ATHENS • TOKYO • MILAN

Harlequin Presents first edition September 1987
ISBN 0-373-11010-3

Original hardcover edition published in 1986
by Mills & Boon Limited

CHAPTER ONE

A CAR door slammed, and high heels clicked across the paving stones with brisk impatience. As the glass doors of the towering office block swung open, the security guard got to his feet, his usually impassive face registering faint surprise.

'Miss Landon—we weren't expecting you back for another ten days ...'

He was left gaping after Ashley Landon's retreating back as it pursued an openly stormy passage to the lift, and with a shrug he returned to his cubicle.

'Someone's for it,' he remarked to no one in particular.

The lift stopped at the sixth floor, and the doors glided open to release the sole passenger. She was a slim girl, slightly above medium height, the sculptured lines of her elegantly bobbed black hair giving emphasis to her pointed chin and high cheekbones. Her clothes were expensive, but sat awkwardly on her body, as if she'd had other things on her mind when she put them on. And the muted beige of her skirt and jacket did nothing for her clear, pale skin, or her green eyes, glinting now like an angry cat's.

When she reached the door marked 'Company Secretary' she flung it open and walked in without knocking with the air of one who has the right, past the startled typist, and straight into the inner office.

Henry Brett was on the telephone, and he looked up frowning at the unceremonious opening of his

door, his face clearing instantly when he saw his
visitor.

He made a swift excuse to his caller, and
replaced his receiver, coming round his desk, hand
outstretched.

'Ashley, my dear, you're back already. That's
wonderful!'

'Hardly the way I'd describe the disruption of my
first vacation in three years,' Ashley rejoined crisply.
'But the signals seemed too urgent to ignore. What
the hell's going on?'

Henry Brett sighed, steering her to a chair. 'A
takeover,' he said succinctly. 'Marshalls are making
yet another bid for our shares.'

'They must be mad,' Ashley said, dropping her
bag to the floor beside her. 'They got a very
conclusive answer the last time they tried it, and
nothing's changed.'

'I'm afraid it has,' Henry said levelly. He pressed
a buzzer on his desk, and spoke into the intercom.
'Jean, could you rustle up some coffee?'

'Not for me,' Ashley cut in.

'I think when you've heard me out, you're going
to need some stimulant,' said Henry, his genial face
sober. 'I can't hide it from you, Ashley. This time
they mean business, and they could succeed.
According to the recent soundings I've been taking,
they could have a majority of our board on their
side.'

There was a brief appalled silence, then Ashley
said, 'Henry, you can't be serious! Why, last time,
every member of the board was solidly one hundred
per cent behind Landons.'

'They were solidly one hundred per cent behind
your father,' Henry said grimly. 'But Silas has been
dead for two years, my dear. And you must

remember that quite apart from the fact that his personality could carry anything through, most of the board owed him a great deal. After all, he'd put the majority of them where they were, and that counted—then.'

'But not any more.' There was a painful constriction in Ashley's throat. 'My God, Henry, I know I'm not my father, and never can be, but I've done my best to run the company exactly as he would have done ...'

'No one would deny that.' Seated on the edge of his desk, Henry sent her a compassionate look. 'You've done everything and more that anyone could expect, but the fact remains ...'

'The fact remains I'm not a man,' Ashley said with a mirthless smile. 'And the board—hidebound traditionalists every one of them—have never believed a woman of my age is capable of running a property development company the size of Landons.'

Henry looked embarrassed. 'Hang it all, Ashley, it was Silas' own view, and you know it.'

'Yes,' she said in a low voice. 'But Henry, I've tried so hard to be the son he wanted—I really have ...'

'No one could have done more,' he assured her warmly. 'But it was a responsibility Silas never wanted you to have. It was that damnfool rule of your grandfather's that only a member of the family could become company chairman that had him hidebound. That was why ...' He stopped in sudden embarrassment. 'Oh, damnation!'

'It's all right, Henry,' Ashley said in a level voice. 'I won't fall apart at the seams if you talk about it. My God, it was over three years ago!'

'All right then,' Henry said quietly. 'That was why he wanted you to marry Jago Marrick. As his son-in-law, Jago would have become chairman after Silas—the strong man at the top the board wanted.'

'Oh, Jago was that all right.' Ashley bit her lip. 'It was as husband material that he failed to meet requirements. But that's all in the past. He's settled in the States now, and probably on his way to his second million.'

'Or even his third,' Henry said wryly. He paused. 'But I'm glad to hear you've managed to put the whole sorry business behind you. I had to think very hard about bringing you home at this time.'

'But why?' She looked at him blankly. 'This is an emergency. Where else would I be?'

Henry cleared his throat. 'You see, there's another factor. Giles Marrick died very suddenly, only a few days after you left for the Caribbean.'

'Jago's cousin?' Ashley frowned. 'I'm sorry. He was a kind man.' She stopped abruptly. 'Oh, I see—Jago came back for the funeral.'

'And not just for the funeral,' said Henry with a trace of heaviness. 'Rumour has it that he intends to stay. He's Giles Marrick's heir, of course, so the Manor and the estate now belongs to him, although I believe the widow has some kind of life interest in it.'

'Yes.' She managed the monosyllable from a taut throat. 'At least, until she remarries.'

'Which probably won't be long,' Henry conceded. 'Good-looking woman, and years younger than Marrick himself, of course.'

'Years,' Ashley agreed quietly. Although Jago had explained the position to her during their brief engagement, it had always cost her a pang to think that when he finally owned the beautiful Georgian house, Erica would still have the right to live there—Erica, with her sultry blonde good looks and malicious tongue.

Mentally, she gave herself a little impatient shake. The Manor was no longer any concern of hers. The loss of Landons was.

She said crisply, 'Don't look so concerned, Henry. I got over Jago a long time ago. Let's get back to the main priority. How did you know Marshalls were sniffing round again?'

'Movement of shares. And then Clive Farnsworth advised me privately that he was being pressed to sell his holding, and warned me that a majority of the board would be in favour of accepting Marshalls' offer.'

'It's unbelievable!' Ashley made a small sound of disgust. 'Why, everyone knows what my father thought of them. He said they were sharks—jerrybuilders creating modern slums.'

'He was right,' Henry said bitterly. 'Which is why they want Landons, of course, to confer a cloak of respectability on their operations. It's the company name they want as well as its assets. But their real ace in the hole is their new managing director, a real dynamo by the sound of him. I gather he reminds some of the older board members of Silas when he was young. That's the enticement—the kind of strong male leadership they're used to.'

'My God, what an attitude!' Ashley expelled her breath in a small harsh sigh. 'It belongs in the Ark.'

'I can't deny that, but we can't dismiss it either.' His gaze met hers squarely. 'We have a real problem here, Ashley. The board aren't just a set of dyed-in-the-wool male chauvinists. They're anxious about our recent performance.'

He broke off as the door opened and Jean Hurst came in with a tray of coffee.

It was what she needed after all, Ashley discovered

wryly, as she accepted a cup of the dark, fragrant brew, and sipped it gratefully.

When they were alone again, she said, 'Was it deliberate? Did Marshalls wait for me to go to Barbados before they made their move?'

Henry looked slightly taken aback. 'It's possible. They must know that loyalty to Silas' memory still exerts quite a hold.'

'So—we fight.' She lifted her chin. 'What am I up against, if it came to a straight boardroom battle?'

'I think you'd just lose,' he admitted, and she winced.

'I can't bear it! To see everything Grandfather and Silas worked for just—handed over to a cowboy outfit like Marshalls. My God, I'd do anything— anything, to stop it happening.'

'I hope you're not contemplating a sex-change,' Henry made a heavy-handed attempt at humour.

Ashley grimaced. 'Coupled with an operation to make me ten years older? Don't tell me that isn't part of the problem.'

'You're just not what they're used to,' Henry said tiredly. 'To most of their generation, women are wives or secretaries, cast in the mould from birth.' He paused. 'And I'm afraid many of them see your—repudiation of your engagement to Jago Marrick as a sign of—feminine instability. They worry that it might break out again some time.'

'Oh, no,' she said with soft bitterness. 'My brush with Jago was a one-off thing—never, I pray, to be repeated.' She put her cup down on the desk. 'When I broke off my engagement, I don't think Silas ever really understood, or forgave me. He thought the end justified the means, and that I was just making a silly fuss about some trivial disagreement. He didn't know ...' She stopped.

'Didn't know what?' Henry prompted sympathetically.

She was silent for a moment, then, 'Didn't know how totally unsuited Jago and I were,' she said stiltedly. She smiled faintly as she got to her feet. 'I'm going home now, Henry. I need to think. But thanks for the timely message. I'd have hated to have been voted out of existence in my absence.'

'That's what I thought,' he said unhappily. 'They're pressing for an emergency board meeting next Thursday. Between now and then I'll see what I can do in the way of persuasion or pressure to change a few minds to our way of thinking.' He sighed. 'But it's going to be an uphill struggle.'

'We'll win,' she said. 'We have to.'

Her words evinced a confidence she didn't feel. Her mood as she drove to her flat was one of dejection.

She'd never envisaged becoming chairman of Landons, but that didn't mean she was prepared to see the company taken away from her.

Oh, Silas, she thought fiercely, why didn't you prepare me better?

Perhaps he would have done, if he'd lived to the ripe old age his bounding energy had seemed to promise. If he hadn't collapsed with a heart attack while exploring a possible site for development, and died in intensive care an hour later, before Ashley could even get to his bedside. Her first act on assuming control of the company had been to complete the deal for the land. Nothing spectacular, but surely a sign to the rest of the world that it was business as usual.

Her flat occupied the top floor of a purpose-built block, which Landons had erected some ten years previously, and was the nearest to a real home she had ever had.

Her mother had, unbelievably, died giving her
birth, and Silas, dazed by grief, had instantly sold
the house they had lived in together. Ashley's
earliest memories were of a changing landscape of
hotel suites, and a shifting population of nannies.
Silas travelled the country, and she, perforce,
travelled with him until she was old enough to be
despatched to boarding school.

She had understood quite early in their relationship that she seemed to make her father uncomfort-
able, and had assumed it was because of some painful
physical resemblance to her mother. Gradually she
came to realise that, whether he was aware of it or
not, Silas resented the fact that his only child was
not the boy he had planned on. Yet he had never
made any attempt to alter the situation by marrying
again, although he had enjoyed various discreet
liaisons over the years, seeming perfectly content
with his nomadic existence, the only awkwardness
occurring when he was obliged to have Ashley with
him.

She had spent many dull hours reading, watching
television, wandering round strange towns, watching
other people's lives from a distance, until at last,
when she was sixteen, she had rebelled, and insisted
on accompanying him on to site. He had been
openly reluctant at first, but when he saw she was
adamant he had acceded, and slowly a new
relationship had been forged between them. He had
started by being sceptical about her interest, but he
answered her questions with total frankness, and
she had learned a great deal simply by being with
him.

But he had been by no means preparing her to
take over from him. His plans for her future had

been very different, as she had suddenly, and painfully, discovered.

In her small elegant bathroom, she stripped and showered slowly, letting the water pour through her hair and down her body. She dried herself without haste, and wrapped in a fresh towel, sarong-style, wandered back to the bedroom and stretched out on her bed.

She felt infinitely weary, but sleep eluded her just the same. There was too much on her mind, she thought, punching the pillow. And if she was honest, the problem about the takeover wasn't foremost in her thoughts as it should have been.

Jago, it seemed, was back, and possibly planning to stay. She had banked very heavily on never having to see him again, but if he was really going to be around as a permanent feature, she didn't see how this could be avoided. It wasn't that large a town. Nor could she leave. This was where Landons had its head office, so she couldn't run, no matter how much she might want to.

Not that there was any logic in that, she castigated herself scornfully. There was no reason why she and Jago should not meet in a perfectly civilised manner. She'd got over that heartbreaking, desperate, adolescent love for him a long time ago. He couldn't hurt her again, so what was she afraid of?

The million-dollar question, Ashley thought ironically.

She bit her lip savagely. As a future wife for a man like Jago Marrick, she'd been a disaster, but as Silas' successor, she thought she had enjoyed a modest success. She had felt desperately isolated at first in her new eminence, but she had listened carefully, and made full use of all the experience and expertise which had been offered.

She sighed. Yet in spite of all her efforts, the board still didn't trust her, or have any real confidence in her, and all her buried insecurities were burrowing to the surface, nagging and gnawing at her mind. She was not quite twenty-two, after all, and not very old to be doing battle for her share of the market place—a fact of which Marshalls were clearly well aware. Their board obviously regarded the present takeover attempt as no contest, and if she was honest, she could see little way of stopping them.

If it was any other company, she thought ruefully. But stories of Marshalls' shoddy dealings and poor workmanship were rife in the industry, and they had already brought a libel action against a well-known satirical magazine which had lambasted them over a new shopping centre, threatened with structural collapse. They had won their case on a technicality, but with derisory damages.

Yet they were still wealthy enough, and endowed with sufficient clout to be bidding for Landons. They knew that their only chance of success was appealing to the inherent greed of human nature. And shareholders, in this respect, were just as human as anyone else.

The sudden trill of the phone beside the bed startled her, and she stared at it resentfully, wishing she'd had the foresight to disconnect it. She waited for the caller to get tired of waiting, and ring off, but it didn't happen. Few people knew she was back, she thought, so perhaps it was Henry calling to apprise her of some new development. And it was clear he wasn't giving up, so she lifted the receiver.

'Hello,' she said grudgingly.

'So you are back.' Jago's voice, low, sardonic,

and totally unmistakable. 'I presumed old Henry would have pushed the panic button by now.'

'I think you have the wrong number,' she said wildly. 'I don't know what you're talking about ...'

'Yes, you do, Ash, so don't play games. According to the hints and rumours in the financial columns, Landons have a serious problem. I think we should talk.'

'Well, I don't.' In spite of herself, her voice sounded ragged, his deliberate diminution of her name rousing memories she would rather have denied. 'I don't need your help.'

'I thought three years might have matured you, Ash,' he jibed at her. 'But it seems you're still the same prickly schoolgirl, nursing your hurt pride. And for that, you're prepared to see Landons go down the drain. You amaze me!'

'That isn't true,' she said stiffly. 'If you have any helpful suggestions, then you should get in touch with Henry. I'm sure he'd be glad to hear from you.'

'Although you're not.' Jago gave a low laugh. 'Well, I suppose that was too much to expect under the circumstances. But you will be hearing from me, Ash, and sooner than you think. I had the greatest admiration for Silas, and I'm not prepared to see his company go to the wall for the sake of past differences between the two of us.'

'I like "past differences",' Ashley said contemptuously. 'It's a good blanket term to cover your mercenary agreement with my father, and your flagrant infidelity!'

'Oh, it covers a damned sight more than that,' he said pleasantly. 'But I'm glad you approve. It's a start anyway. I'll be seeing you, then.' The line disconnected briskly.

He had never, Ashley thought, as she replaced her own receiver, been one for prolonged farewells.

She sat up, nervously hitching up her towel, as though Jago was in the room with her, his tawny hazel eyes observing her state of disarray with that overt sensuality which had so disturbed her during their brief, ill-fated relationship.

He'd called her a prickly schoolgirl, and she supposed he had a certain amount of justification, remembering how she had nervously shied away from any physical advances he'd made to her. Not even the fact that she had fallen head over heels in love with him had been able to mitigate her panic-stricken recoil from any real intimacy between them during their engagement.

And if she had been frightened by the unknown passions she had sensed were tightly leashed in his lean male body, then she had been utterly terrified by the wild unbidden reaction of her own innocent flesh to his lightest touch. And there was no one to help her understand or cope with these new and overwhelming sensations. The sex education lessons at her school had described the mechanics, but said nothing about the emotions which should accompany such experiences, and Ashley's housemistress had given muddled, embarrassed talks about the problems inherent in 'leading men on', quoting current rape statistics, and advising 'keeping oneself decent for marriage'.

And Silas' values, she had discovered when she had nerved herself to mention the topic to him, were equally rigid. Purity was what a man looked for in his future wife, he had told her flatly, and she could learn anything she needed to know from her husband when the time came.

When Jago held her close, she felt totally

confused, her body at war with her mind, which insisted that such an intensity of emotion must be wrong, even in some way abnormal.

Eventually, it seemed easier to keep Jago at arms' length. Or at any rate simpler, she amended hastily, because it had never been easy.

She had supposed naïvely that Silas was right, and that once they were married everything would be different. That wearing Jago's ring, having the right to call herself his wife, would bring about some fundamental sea-change in her. Only she had never had the opportunity to find out.

The wedding had only been a few weeks away when she had finally found out the truth about the kind of man she was marrying. She hadn't seen Jago for several days, not since they'd spent an evening at the theatre together. Afterwards, he had suggested she go back to his flat with him for a nightcap, and she had shrunk immediately. It was altogether too secluded and intimate an environment for her to cope with, feeling as she did, and she'd heard herself babbling some feeble excuse. That Jago had recognised it as such was evident, although he had said nothing. But his mouth had tightened, and he had driven her home with almost exaggerated care, depositing her on her doorstep with chilly courtesy, not even bothering to bestow the most chaste of goodnight kisses.

Ashley told herself he was being unreasonable, and that she wasn't going to be the first to make amends, but as time passed without a word from him, her need for reassurance got the better of her pride, and she tried to telephone him. When there was no reply from the flat, she told herself he was probably staying at the Manor, as Giles liked him to do from time to time.

But when she drove out to the Manor that evening, she found only Erica Marrick at home. She was sitting in the big drawing room, stitching at a piece of tapestry set up in a frame in front of her, and Ashley, who had no skill at sewing, watched in fascination as the needle pierced the canvas over and over again.

Later, when Ashley allowed herself to recall that terrible evening and its aftermath, she was to remember above all that shining needle, stabbing in and out, and feel as if it was her own flesh that it was wounding.

'I'm sorry you've had a wasted journey,' Erica said, when the usual social pleasantries had been observed. 'It might have been wiser to ring first, and check where he was.'

Ashley forbore to mention that she'd been trying to contact Jago for two days. She said, trying to sound casual, 'I suppose you've no idea where he could be?'

Erica chose another strand of thread. 'None at all, my dear. Giles is only Jago's cousin, not his keeper. Jago's an adult male. He comes and goes here as he chooses, and we don't ask any indiscreet questions. Much the best way, I assure you.' She threaded her needle. 'Jago doesn't actually live here yet.'

'I know,' Ashley said huskily. 'But I thought—I got the impression he was spending more time here these days—using the flat rather less.'

'I hardly think so.' The needle stabbed again. 'After all, it's the one small piece of bachelor independence which hasn't been eroded yet, and he'll be anxious to hang on to that as long as possible, I would imagine. He's sacrificed quite a lot already,' she added almost casually. 'I hope he finds Landons is worth it.'

Ashley's brows drew together. 'I don't quite understand ...'

'How wise of you,' purred Erica. 'It's always so much better to respect the conventions in these matters, and pretend the marriage has been arranged—such a telling phrase, I always think—for personal rather than business reasons.'

Ashley felt as if a hand was slowly tightening round her throat. 'Are you insinuating that Jago is marrying me only to gain a stake in Landons?'

'Hardly a stake, my dear.' The deadly needle went in and out, doing its work. 'After all, you're an only child with neither the physical nor mental capacity to become a—a captain of industry. Your father, naturally, needs someone he can trust to run the company eventually, and who better than a son-in-law and as you were—gratifyingly ready to marry him, and Jago is extremely ambitious, everyone's satisfied.'

There was a silence. Ashley said flatly, 'I don't believe you.'

Erica laughed. 'Of course not. Why should you? And you have nothing to worry about. Jago will never forget that you're Daddy's daughter, and be less than attentive, but you must remember to allow him—a little leeway now, before the noose tightens for ever. So why don't you go home like a good girl, and wait for him to call you. I'm sure he will, eventually. He tends to have a fairly strict sense of duty,' she added blandly.

Some guardian angel must have protected Ashley on that nightmare drive to his flat, because she remembered nothing about it.

All the way there, a voice in her head was whispering, 'It can't be true—can't be true ...'

And yet suspicion, once planted, was growing like a weed in the sun, sending out deadly tentacles to smother and choke. She had to see Jago, to confront him, and find out once and for all the real truth behind their marriage.

Because, she had to admit, the romance had been a whirlwind affair. She hadn't seen a great deal of Jago while she was growing up, but after Silas had decided to seek a permanent home base near the company headquarters, they had begun to come into contact with each other.

At first, she had been full of shy admiration, gauche and tongue-tied whenever he was around. As he shared her father's professional interests, it was inevitable that they should meet. Sometimes he was kind to her, at others, he teased her unmercifully. Gradually, almost in spite of herself, her admiration turned to a kind of hero-worship, and then, bewilderingly, to something much deeper.

Ashley had found she was aching for a glimpse of him, and agonising when this was denied her. She was ecstatic when he noticed her—once he gave her a lift home from the library, and she lived on it for weeks—and miserable when the passenger seat in his car was filled by one of the leggy blondes he seemed to favour. Not that he was always at home by any means. A lot of the time he was away, pursuing his career, immersed in one of the civil engineering projects for which he had trained at university.

'He's going straight to the top, that lad,' Silas had remarked more than once with unveiled satisfaction.

But Jago's ambitions and professional abilities counted for little with Ashley. For her, he was the focus of all her romantic dreams, and when, right

out of the blue, he had rung and invited her to
have dinner with him, she had thought she would
die of delight.

But she had lived, and it was the start of an
idyllic period in her life. Jago dined her, and danced
with her, partnering her at tennis, taking her on
picnics, and visits to the theatre and cinema.

And when, after six heady weeks, he had asked
her to marry him, she had said 'Yes' eagerly, with
no thought of dissimulation. 'Gratifyingly ready,'
Erica had said mockingly, she recalled with a shiver
of nausea. But it was no more than the truth. She'd
been foolishly, blindly ready to allow herself to be
handed over in exchange for the Landon empire.

As she drove, a lot of pieces seemed to be coming
together in an increasingly terrifying pattern. She
remembered the impatience in him, coiled like a
spring, when she had drawn back from the growingly
explicit demands of his mouth and hands, so
different from the gentle restraint he had displayed
during the early days of their courtship.

Before he was sure of her, said a small icy voice
in her brain.

If he'd really cared for her, wouldn't he
have been prepared to make allowances for her
inexperience? she asked herself.

And more troubling still, he had never actually
said in so many words that he loved her. He wanted
to make love to her, in any way she would permit,
but all he had said when she agreed to be his wife,
was, 'Darling Ash, I'll try and make you happy.'

She'd been more than content with that at the
time, but now it seemed a disturbing omission.

At first when she rang the doorbell at his flat, she
thought he was still out somewhere, and she was
just about to turn away in defeat when she heard

the sound of movement inside.

The door opened, and they faced each other. He looked terrible, was her first thought. He was pale, and his eyes were bloodshot, and he seemed to be wearing a dressing gown, and nothing else.

She said anxiously, 'Jago, are you ill?' She took a step forward, to be arrested by the sour reek of spirits on his breath. It was something she hadn't encountered before with him, and it alarmed her.

In his turn, he was staring at her as if he didn't know who she was, and then she saw a dawning horror in his eyes.

And in the same instant heard a girl's voice saying with plaintive impatience, 'Sweetie, aren't you ever coming back to bed? Get rid of whoever it is and ...' She appeared from the bedroom, wearing nothing but the coverlet from the bed draped round her, none too effectively.

The hand was round Ashley's throat again, tightening, squeezing ...

The girl came forward to Jago's side. Her eyes, blue and hard as nails, flicked over Ashley dismissively.

'They say three's a crowd, don't they, darling? Or is that the way you like it?'

Jago slumped against the door jamb with a muffled groan.

Ashley wanted to stamp her feet. She wanted to kick, to lash out with her hands, and tear with her nails, and scream. She wanted to damage them, both of them, physically. Mark them as they had smashed her emotionally.

Nausea rose, hot and acrid, in her throat, and she turned and ran down the stairs, not waiting for the lift, and out into the chill of the night air. She leaned against her car, retching miserably, uncaring who might see her or what conclusions they might draw. Then, as soon as she was sufficiently in control of herself, she climbed into the driving seat, and started the engine. She didn't go home. She drove out of town, and down to the river, parking in the very spot where Jago had proposed to her, sitting white-faced and burning-eyed until dawn.

When she finally returned home, she brushed aside her father's reproaches and anxious queries, saying merely that she'd had some thinking to do, and needed to be alone. When she'd added that she was no longer going to marry Jago she and Silas had the worst row of their lives.

'But you can't throw him over for some whim!' he'd raged at her. 'My God, girl, only last week you thought the sun, moon, and stars all shone out of him! And I need him. I need a strong man to run Landons after I'm gone. As your husband he can become chairman after me. As soon as I met him, I knew he was the right man.'

'Right for me?' she wanted to ask, wincing. 'Or merely right for Landons?' But she'd never voiced the query.

Her magnificent solitaire diamond ring she'd sent back to Jago by company messenger, with a note stating bleakly that she never wanted to see him or hear from him again.

And nor had she, Ashley thought wearily, until now. Until that phone call, like a bolt from the blue.

Not only was her company at risk. With Jago's return, her precarious peace of mind was threatened. And that, frighteningly, seemed a great deal worse.

CHAPTER TWO

AFTER a while, when she felt a little calmer, she lifted the telephone and dialled.

'Martin Witham, please,' she told the receptionist who answered. 'Tell him Miss Landon is calling.'

She was put through with flattering promptness.

'Ashley!' Martin sounded pleased and surprised. 'Why on earth are you back so soon?'

'Clearly, you haven't been reading the financial pages,' she said lightly. 'Let's just say a state of emergency's been declared and it seemed better to return.'

'My poor sweet!' His voice was warm and concerned. 'Want to tell me all about it over dinner at the Country Club tonight?'

She laughed. 'That's exactly what I hoped you'd say,' she teased. 'Pick me up at eight?'

'I'll be counting the minutes,' he promised.

She felt better after that. His voice had reassured her, helping to take away the sour taste the earlier call had left.

She'd been seeing Martin for a couple of months, since he'd arrived from London to join a local firm of solicitors. After Jago, Ashley had tended to steer clear of any kind of involvement, but Martin had persuaded her to think again, although he had made it clear from the first that he was in no hurry to rush into any kind of serious relationship. He'd been divorced, he told her, and was still licking his wounds, but he would be glad of some female companionship.

It was an arrangement which suited them both very well. Since Silas' death, Ashley had been lonelier than she cared to remember, and Martin's friendship had buoyed her up, just when she needed it most.

And she needed him now, she thought ruefully.

Martin had not told her very much about his marriage, and she was equally reticent on the subject of her broken engagement. Now, she supposed, she would have to tell Martin that her ex-fiancé was back in town, throwing fresh attention on an episode she had hoped was behind her for ever.

She felt depression closing in on her like a cloud, and gave herself a swift mental shake. Sleep was what she needed, and food. She made herself an omelette in her compact kitchen, eating every scrap, then curled up on the living room sofa, emptying her mind, and relaxing her muscles until her intrinsic weariness had its way with her.

When she woke, she felt perceptibly better, refreshed and even relaxed. Which seemed, she thought, to bode well for the evening ahead. She applied her usual light make-up, sprayed herself lavishly with *Amazone*, then zipped herself into a new dress she'd bought on impulse during her West Indian holiday. It was the colour which had attracted her originally—a clear, vivid emerald, enhancing her eyes.

Her one beauty, she thought critically, as she turned and twisted in front of the mirror, trying to decide whether the dress was too extreme for the sedate delights of the County Club. Certainly, the crossover bodice plunged lower than anything she had worn before, and the back of the dress bared

her from the brief halter round her neck almost to
the base of her spine. For a moment, she was
tempted to change into something more demure,
something that reflected the muted businesslike
image she tried to project these days. Then she
tossed her head, making her glossy hair swing
challengingly.

To hell with it, she thought recklessly. Since the
night of Jago's betrayal, she'd lived a kind of half-
life. Perhaps it was only right that his return
should signal her emergence from her self-imposed
chrysalis—proclaiming to the world at large, as well
as himself, that she no longer carried even the
flicker of a torch for him.

She'd been a fool to react like that to his call, she
told herself angrily. She should have been civil but
indifferent, instead of letting him know he could
still get under her skin. Well, she would know
better at their next encounter—if there was one.

Martin's expression when she admitted him to the
flat was evidence, if she needed it, that her change
of image was a success. And it reminded her too of
how little thought she'd given to her appearance
over the past couple of years.

'The new me,' she explained. 'Do you approve?'

'I'm not sure if "approve" is the word I'm looking
for,' Martin said carefully. 'May I kiss you, or will
it spoil your make-up?'

Ashley went readily into his arms. She was
accustomed to the light embraces they exchanged on
meeting and parting, and when Martin deliberately
prolonged and deepened the kiss, she made no
demur. Perhaps it wasn't just the outer shell she
needed to change, she thought, submitting passively
to the ardent pressure of his mouth on hers.

She waited for some answering surge in her own

blood, but it didn't happen. Probably she was still too tired and caught off-balance by the past twenty-four hours to be able to conjure up much of a response, she excused herself, as they left for the Club.

It was already quite crowded when they arrived. Martin had booked a corner table, away from the dance floor where a three-piece band played quietly.

'The usual wide choice, I see,' he said wryly, handing her a menu. 'Steak, steak, scampi or steak.'

Ashley smiled at him. 'And I keep telling you that's the height of sophistication in this neck of the woods,' she teased. ·

'So you do,' he muttered. 'What's it to be, then?'

'Melon, please, followed by a fillet steak rare to medium, and a side salad.'

'And I'll have the same,' Martin told the waiter. His hand reached for Ashley's across the table. 'We never seem to ask for anything else. Maybe we should make it a standing order.'

'Maybe,' Ashley returned neutrally. She returned the pressure of his fingers, but his words troubled her, seeming to signal a permanence she wasn't ready for. She was relieved when the conversation took a less personal turn. Martin was engaged in litigation work, and he gave a droll description of some of the cases he'd been defending while she way away.

Ashley leaned back in her chair, enjoying the fragrance of the white wine she had asked for as an aperitif, her eyes idly scanning the room as she did so.

'And when the magistrate asked if he had anything to say, the idiot came back with "But the car always stalls if I drive at less than sixty, Your Worship",' Martin was saying, then his voice sharpened.

'Ashley, what is it? Are you all right?'

Her whole body had tensed, and she could feel the blood draining from her face. Standing in the doorway, looking round the room, was Jago Marrick.

Her first, instinctive thought was how little he had changed in the intervening years. The breach between them had left no mark on him as it had on her, but then why should it? she asked herself bitterly. No doubt he'd regretted the loss of Landons, but he was a success in his own right as Silas had always predicted. Ashley had been nothing more to him than a means to an end.

But it was unfair, she thought, digging her nails into the palms of her hands, that his physical appeal should not have diminished. Outwardly, he was still the man she'd fallen so helplessly in love with.

The lean, graceful body, the lightly curling brown hair, still worn rather longer than convention demanded, the cool, incisive lines of nose, mouth and jaw, had lost none of their impact, thrusting her into sudden unwelcome turmoil.

With a superlative effort she fought for control.

'It's all right,' she said, forcing a little laugh, and inwardly thankful for the comparative seclusion of their table. 'I—I'm jet-lagged still, I suppose. Perhaps I should have had a quiet evening at home.'

'Well, you still can,' Martin assured her promptly. 'When we've eaten, I'll drive you back.' He smiled at her. 'Some cosseting's what you need.'

She doubted whether she needed anything he had in mind but now was not the time to be talking about that. She felt suddenly like an animal, caught in a snare with the hunter drawing closer ...

Get a grip on yourself, she adjured herself, silently and savagely. So he's here. It's a public place, and he has as much right to use it as you.

But there's nothing he can do to you any more—nothing ...

Martin said with a faint groan, 'Oh, hell! One of the firm's most important clients has just come in, and he's heading this way. I shall have to be civil at least.'

Ashley knew with a sense of sick inevitability who it would be, and nerved herself, her hands clenching into fists in her lap, her face schooled to impassivity.

'Good evening, Witham.' Jago stopped beside their table. She made herself look up, her face stretched into a polite smile which felt like a grimace. He wasn't alone, she saw. Erica was beside him, ethereal in black chiffon, clinging to his arm. The grieving widow's first public appearance, Ashley decided ironically.

Jago was looking at her now, his brows lifting with faint cynicism as he assimilated her appearance.

'Ashley,' he said softly. 'What a charming surprise.'

'You know each other?' asked Martin. 'I was just about to introduce you.'

'No need,' Jago assured him. 'Ashley and I are old—acquaintances, aren't we, darling?'

'You could say that,' she said shortly. She looked past him to Erica. 'Please accept my condolences on your sad loss, Mrs Marrick.'

'Such a terrible shock,' Erica sighed delicately. 'But life must go on. That's what dear Giles would have wanted.'

Remembering the big, bluff man with his booming laugh, Ashley thought this was probably true. At any rate, it absolved Erica from most of the conventions of mourning, she decided cynically.

'Won't you join us?' Martin offered, to Ashley's

horror.

'We'd be delighted,' Jago said smoothly, and she
had to bite back a gasp of sheer anguish. But
nothing could be done; a waiter was already hurrying
to lay two extra covers. Ashley's sole consolation
was that Erica seemed no better pleased by the
situation than she was herself, judging by the
expression she had seen fleetingly cross the widow's
lovely face, and the way her fingers were curving
possessively on Jago's sleeve.

Well, everyone looks for consolation in their own
way, she told herself, and turned an artificially
radiant smile on Martin.

The meal was a three-dimensional, Technicolored
nightmare, with full stereophonic sound. The steaks,
when they arrived, were excellent, but Ashley might
just as well have been chewing her way through an
old handbag for all the enjoyment she derived from
hers. Tautly, she declined a dessert when it was
offered, and coffee too, praying that Martin would
take the hint, and whisk her away as he'd promised.

But Martin wasn't in the market for hints.
Oblivious to any undercurrents, he was leaning back
in his chair, being expansive and thoroughly enjoying
himself. Taking the opportunity to impress an
important client, Ashley thought, then chided herself
for being unkind.

She glanced up, and found Jago's eyes on her.
He, she realised resentfully, wasn't even making an
attempt at pretence. Openly and unashamedly, he
was staring at her, insolently studying the shape of
her breasts under the flimsy bodice, and to her
shame and horror she found her body reacting to
the calculation of his gaze, the nipples hardening
and thrusting against the soft cling of the fabric.
And, worst of all, she could tell by the slow smile

curling his firm-lipped mouth that her involuntary arousal had not gone unnoticed.

Mortified beyond all bearing, she stared down at the table. What kind of person was she to allow herself to be excited by a look from a man who had treated her as badly as Jago had done? She swallowed, remembering that he had always had that effect on her, no matter how hard she'd tried to resist it. Even in company, one lingering glance from him had been enough to melt her bones, and send sweet fire coursing through her veins. It was only later, alone with him, that the problems had started, shame at her body's own urgency freezing her into frightened rigidity when he tried to kiss and caress her.

But that was something she neither needed nor wanted to remember, and she tried to turn her attention elsewhere, gazing at the couples moving round the dance floor in time to the music.

Jago leaned towards her. 'Would you like to dance?' he asked courteously.

Her voice was stony. 'No, thank you.'

'Oh, go on, darling,' Martin urged jovially. 'You know you love this tune.'

Had she really admitted that to him? she asked herself despairingly. How could she—when it was a song she'd danced to with Jago over and over again in those first heady days?

'Then that settles it.' Jago was standing beside her chair, reaching for her hand, drawing her inexorably to her feet before she could utter any further protest.

She couldn't free herself without making some kind of scene, and her spirit quailed at the thought of that, so numbly she allowed him to guide her through the encircling tables to the dance floor.

'I'll try not to touch any bare skin,' he said sardonically, as he drew her into his arms. 'But the design of your dress makes it rather difficult.'

She flushed angrily. 'Don't!'

'Why so sensitive?' he jeered. 'You can't help being the way you are, any more than I can. And you certainly never wanted to be touched—by me, at any rate.'

Ashley shrugged, trying not to flinch from the clasp of his cool fingers, making herself move to the music with him. 'Why drag up the past?' she asked shortly. 'It was a long time ago. I've changed. Probably we both have.'

'In your case, the change is formidable,' he said softly. 'What's brought about this new sophistication? Witham?'

'Perhaps,' said Ashley, lifting her chin. 'If it's any of your business.'

The tawny eyes glittered down at her. 'Going to marry him, Ash?'

'Now that really is none of your business.' Ashley bit her lip. 'I'd like to go back to the table, please.'

'When the dance is over.' He swung her round, gently but inexorably, making her realise it was impossible to be free without undignified hassle. 'And isn't it natural that I should be interested in your plans for the future? After all, they once involved me quite intimately, if you recall.'

'I'm not likely to forget,' she said scornfully. 'I'd have said you'd totally forfeited any right to enquire into my private life. And while we're on the subject, how did you get hold of my phone number? I'm ex-directory.'

'Let's say a little bird told me,' he said. 'You seem rather besieged at the moment. I thought you might welcome a friendly call.'

'Then you miscalculated,' Ashley said bitingly. 'I don't need your interest in my affairs, business or personal. In future, kindly leave me alone.'

Jago gave her a meditative look, his eyes hooded. 'That isn't as easy as it sounds. I'd say we were bound to run into each other in a place this size. Don't you think we should at least practise being civil to each other?'

Ashley tried to quell the inner dismay his words evoked. He seemed to be confirming that he would not, after all, be returning to the States, just as Henry had suggested.

'It's a small town indeed,' she said.' And rather limiting, I'd have thought, for someone of your ambition. I imagine you can't wait to go back to America.'

'Then your imagination is playing you tricks,' he said pleasantly. 'I'll be happy to discuss my plans with you, Ashley, but now is not the time. I didn't ask you to dance in order to have a serious talk.'

'No? Then I can only assume you intended to annoy me.' She shook her head. 'I'm sorry, Jago. The most I can call on where you're concerned is indifference. If anyone's suffering from any kind of aggravation here tonight, then it's probably your cousin Erica.'

'Oh, I think Witham is managing to keep her entertained,' he said casually. 'Although he's a bit of a dull stick.'

'He's a decent person,' Ashley said levelly. 'Although I suppose decency is a quality that couldn't be expected to have much appeal for you.'

'Or to you, my sweet vixen.' His mouth curled. 'But I asked you to dance, Ashley, to find out if the change in you is any more than skin deep.' His hand at her back increased its pressure suddenly,

forcing her towards him across the slight decorous
distance that separated them. Bringing her body
into intimate, objectionable contact with his.

Ashley gasped, her eyes flashing green fire at
him, as she tried unavailingly to pull away. Her lips
parted in a protest which was fated never to be
uttered as Jago's mouth came down on hers, warm,
firm, and shamelessly sensual.

Her senses reeled under the suddenness of the
onslaught. Her body seemed to be melting, her legs
no longer able to support her properly, the blood in
her veins moving slowly, thick and sweet as honey,
as she fought for control.

The kiss seemed endless and she had to curb the
instinct to yield, to respond, to explore his mouth
as avidly as he was seeking the secrets of hers. It
was a temptation that had to be resisted at all costs,
and she knew it, even though her body was
overwhelmed, trembling with the surge of unsatisfied
longing within her.

But she had to remember that he cared no more
for her now than he had three years ago, a small
desperate voice in her head warned her. He was
trying to score points, that was all. To let the eyes
watching them know that the breach between them,
once a nine-day wonder, was either healed or no
longer important.

When at last he took his mouth from hers, it was
with open reluctance. The music had stopped, and
only a smattering of applause from the other dancers
filled the amazed and questioning silence around
them.

Still dazed, Ashley let Jago lead her back to the
table, aware of the barrage of fascinated and curious
looks and murmured remarks following them. She
was aware too that the couple awaiting them at

their table didn't share that general fascination and curiosity. Martin looked bemused and sullen, and Erica was plainly furious, although she was smiling graciously enough.

Muttering an excuse, Ashley grabbed her bag, and made her way to the refuge of the powder room. Luckily it was deserted, and she sank down on one of the padded stools in front of the mirror and stared at herself. Her eyes looked twice their normal size, and she hadn't a scrap of colour left. She touched the bare, swollen outline of her mouth with fingers that shook slightly.

Jago had made no concessions at all, either to the passage of time which had separated them, or to the fact they were in a public place. His behaviour, by any standard, was unforgivable. She opened her bag, fumbling a little as she retrieved her compact and lipstick and tried to repair some of the damage he had wrought, while shame and anger built up inside her.

How dare he behave like that! she raged inwardly. His arrogance was appalling. But so, honesty reminded her, had been her own reaction.

She couldn't go back in the dining room, she thought restlessly, to face the stares and speculation, and Jago's silent triumph. She would have to get a message to Martin, telling him she had a headache and wanted to go home.

But when she emerged, she found Martin waiting for her.

She pinned on a smile. 'Ready to go?'

'More than ready.' His voice was pettish, and she smothered a sigh. His hand gripped her elbow almost painfully as they walked to the car park, but he said nothing more until they were in the car, and on their way.

Then, 'What was that all about?' he wanted to know restively.

'Do we have to discuss it now?' Ashley stared in front of her.

'I'd say so. I don't appreciate being made to look a fool in public.'

'If it's any consolation, I don't think that was the main intention.' Ashley bit her lip. 'Jago was trying to—prove a point, and he chose a rather drastic way of doing it, that's all.'

'Old acquaintances, he said.' Martin's mouth turned down at the corners. 'It seemed more than that to me.'

His tone demanded an explanation. Ashley hesitated for a moment, then said reluctantly, 'As it happens, Jago Marrick was the man I was engaged to a couple of years ago.'

'Good God!' Martin, always the most careful of drivers, actually took her eyes off the road to gaze at her while he assimilated the information. 'I hadn't the slightest idea ...'

Ashley sighed. 'I thought someone would probably have mentioned it.'

'I suppose everyone assumed you would have told me yourself.' Martin sounded injured. 'Didn't you think I'd want to know you'd been—involved with one of our top clients?'

Ashley looked down at her interlaced fingers. 'Frankly it was a period of my life I preferred to put out of my mind altogether. Jago was in America, and Giles Marrick could have lived for another thirty years, as far as I knew.' She moistened her lips with the tip of her tongue. 'But what does it matter, anyway? It's over, and has been for a long time.'

After a long pause, Martin said carefully, 'A

casual observer tonight might query that.'

Ashley forced a smile. 'I think tonight was a cross between Jago's idea of a joke, and his wish to tell the world. there's no longer any bad feeling between us.'

'And is that the case?'

She bent her head in affirmation, trying to push out of her mind the memory of that cynically passionate kiss, and her unsought reaction to it.

He said judiciously, 'Well, it's never easy to get over these things, as I know to my cost. Were you very much in love with him, darling?'

'I'm not sure I even knew what love was,' Ashley said tonelessly.

He seemed content with that, and to her relief, didn't insist on accompanying her into the flat as she had half-feared. He accepted her excuse that she was still dog-tired after her flight, and went off, promising tenderly to phone her the next day.

Ashley fell into bed like an automaton, but still she couldn't sleep. She lay for what seemed like hours, staring into the darkness. Didn't she have enough problems? Jago's re-entry into her life was a complication she didn't need.

Or perhaps the trouble she felt brewing through him was simply a figment of her overcharged imagination. He had his own life and responsibilities now, with Erica not the least of them, judging by tonight's showing. He wouldn't have time, let alone the inclination to bait his ex-fiancée.

Surely their lives could run on parallel lines, never crossing the path of each other. And on this comforting reflection, she finally dozed off.

She was woken the next morning by the prolonged ringing of her doorbell. Groggily, she pushed back the covers and grabbed for her robe, trying through the clouds of sleep to remember if the milkman needed paying.

As she opened the door, she stiffened, her whole body taut with outrage as she recognised her visitor.

'You again!' she exclaimed furiously, and tried to slam the door in his face, but Jago was too quick for her. His arm clamped round her waist, lifting her totally off her feet as he stepped into the narrow hall. As he set her down again, the door was already closed behind him.

Ashley gritted between her teeth, 'There's really no end to your presumption! May I know how you discovered my address—or have I the same little bird to thank?'

Jago tutted. 'You sound very crotchety, my sweet. I don't think late nights agree with you. Are you alone, or should I lurk discreetly in the sitting room while Witham makes his escape?'

'If there's any vanishing to be done, you'll do it,' she said tersely. 'Get out!'

'When I've said what I came to say.' The hazel eyes looked her over mockingly. 'Or did you think last night was all there was to it?'

'It seemed more than enough for me,' Ashley snapped. She caught sight of the long case clock in the corner. 'My God,' she said falteringly, 'it isn't even eight o'clock yet! What the hell ...'

Jago produced a carrier bag, 'I thought we'd have a working breakfast,' he said briskly.

'You thought what?' Words failed her.

'A working breakfast,' he repeated kindly. 'They have a lot of them in the States. I'm supplying the food.'

'Well, don't expect me to cook it. I never eat breakfast anyway.'

'Then you should.' He gave her another more

searching look, and her hands moved instinctively to tighten the already secure sash of her robe. 'It occurred to me last night, you can't afford to lose any more weight. Will you show me where the kitchen is, or shall I find it by trial and error?'

'You'll get out of here now!' Ashley raged. 'And take your lousy food with you!'

'Your ways of expressing yourself don't seem to have improved over the years,' Jago said coolly. 'The food is fresh—grapefruit, eggs and bacon, and bread for toast. You don't have to lift a finger. Just eat—and listen to what I have to say.'

'There's nothing you have to talk about that I want to hear.' Eyes sparkling ominously, she faced him, her head held proudly high.

'Not even when the subject under discussion is Landons—and its questionable future?' he asked.

'There is no question about Landons' future,' Ashley denied sharply.

'Now there we differ,' he said quite gently. 'I'd say that without some pretty fancy footwork on your part, Marshalls are going to snap you up, and cheap at the price. Is that what you want?'

'Of course not,' she said impatiently. 'But it's no concern of yours.'

'It's my concern.' There was no amusement in his face. The hazel eyes were cold and inimical as they rested on her. 'Silas was my good friend, remember?'

'I'm hardly likely to forget. I've often thought it a pity you couldn't marry him yourself.'

'And I've often thought it a pity you weren't smacked, as a child, until you couldn't sit down for a week,' Jago said bitingly. 'Now go and get dressed, unless you want to spend the morning in that travesty of a dressing gown. I'll call you when the food's ready.'

She said shakily, 'If I were a man, I'd throw you out.'

'Don't be silly, Ash.' He tapped her hot cheek lightly with his forefinger. 'If you were a man, I wouldn't be here, period.'

She wanted to tell him not to call her 'Ash', but it suddenly seemed infinitely safer to go to her room, and put some clothes on as he'd suggested.

She dragged on jeans, not new, and a sweater which had seen better days, dragging a comb ruthlessly through her black hair. Cosmetics she left severely alone. Jago was not to think she had taken any trouble with her appearance on his account, she told herself vehemently.

The kitchen was full of the scent and crackle of frying bacon and percolating coffee, and in spite of her anger, Ashley's nose twitched in appreciation as she entered. Jago was standing by the hob, slicing tomatoes. He too was wearing jeans, she noticed, the close-fitting denim accentuating the length of his legs and the leanness of his hips. The cuffs of his shirt were unbuttoned and turned casually back revealing tanned forearms. He made her trim kitchen seem cramped, Ashley thought resentfully as she unwillingly took a seat at the small breakfast bar.

'Here.' He poured coffee into a mug and pushed it across the worktop to her.

'Thank you,' she acknowledged stiffly.

'And three bags full to you.' He gave her a long look. 'Unless you relax your attitude, lady, and fast, we're going to get nowhere.'

'Well, that suits me down to the ground,' said Ashley coldly. 'As I haven't the slightest wish to make any kind of progress with you.'

'So, hurt pride and resentment still rule, O.K.

You aren't prepared to swallow either or both for the sake of Landons?'

'I'd give whatever I had to in order to save the company,' Ashley retorted. 'I've already given the last couple of years of my life. Apparently for some of the board, this isn't enough. I don't know what more they want—blood, presumably.'

'No,' he said, 'I think they want the assurance that Landons will continue to be the dynamic, thrusting concern that Silas made it.'

'You seem very well informed,' said Ashley coldly, gritting her teeth, as she complied with his signal to start on her grapefruit. 'Perhaps you're also aware that Landons had a record profit last year.'

'That's true,' he admitted. 'But accrued from the projects that Silas set up. You've kept the company ticking over, and you've delivered the goods, as no one could wish to deny. But your forward planning is lousy. There've been a number of tenders you should have gone for—and got—but haven't. Silas went out and sold Landons in the market place. He was the arch-instigator of all time. Those new civic buildings in town were a case in point. The council never thought on that scale until Silas sold them the idea. Now no one can imagine how they ever did without them. And you can repeat that story over and over again up and down the length of the country.'

'We have plenty of work,' Ashley protested indignantly.

'For the time being—but how much of it is new? How many of your present contracts have you fought for and won?' He shook his head. 'This is what concerns the majority of the board, Ashley, and in their place, I'd probably share that concern.'

Ashley bit her lip, looking with disfavour at the plate he was setting in front of her. 'I can't possibly eat all that,' she protested.

'You'll eat it if I have to hold your nose and force-feed you,' Jago told her forthrightly. 'You're going to need all your strength, lady, and besides, we have other more important issues to argue about than food.' He took his place beside her and began to eat with relish as she registered with annoyance. His presence in her flat, his intrusion into her life was an outrage, but he seemed unconscious of the fact.

'So why are you interfering?' she asked sulkily, cutting into her bacon, and noting crossly that it was done to a crisp, just as she liked it. 'I suppose you've come here to give me some good advice. Well, let me tell you, I don't need ...'

'Mere advice won't get you out of the hole you're in.' He reached for a piece of toast. 'I think the situation calls for rather more drastic action.'

'And you, of course, know exactly how to cope with the crisis,' she said derisively.

'I could get rid of Marshalls for starters.' Jago bit into his toast.

'How?' His confidence needled her.

He sighed. 'By persuading the board to reject their offer.'

Ashley put down her knife and fork. 'But why should they do any such thing, particularly on your say-so?' she demanded heatedly. 'My God, you're not even a member of the Landons board!'

'But I could be.' The hazel eyes looked coolly and directly into hers. 'In fact I could be chairman— if you and I were married.'

CHAPTER THREE

IN a voice she hardly recognised as her own, Ashley gasped 'That—has to be the most insane idea I've ever heard!'

'On the contrary, it makes a lot of sense.' He even had the gall to go on eating, she realised dazedly. 'Think about it, and try using your head, instead of your hormones. It was what Silas always intended, after all.'

'I'm only too well aware of that,' she said rigidly. 'It was a very nice, businesslike arrangement for you both, until you allowed your other—proclivities to get in the way.'

'Ah,' Jago said softly, 'I thought we wouldn't get far before that thorny subject was dragged kicking and screaming into the light of day. You never gave me a chance to explain at the time. Perhaps now you might allow me a few words.'

'The fewer the better.' Suddenly she was hurting again, every image from that terrible night etched on to her memory in agonising detail. 'Although I fail to see what possible explanation you can come up with for your conduct.' She paused theatrically. 'Ah, I know. The lady was your long-lost sister—or your maiden aunt twice removed seeking shelter for the night. Is that how it was?'

'No,' he said, his mouth curling. 'The situation was exactly as you read it. And before you ask— no, she wasn't an old flame, either. I'd picked her up in a bar earlier in the evening. Satisfied?'

'Please spare me the sordid details,' Ashley said scornfully. 'I don't want to hear them.'

'What did you want to hear, I wonder?' he asked cynically. 'Some cosy lie, designed to make you feel better, and whitewash the whole incident? Not a chance. I offered an explanation for what it's worth, but no excuses.'

'There is no possible excuse for what you did,' she said bitterly. 'And you have no right to walk back into my life, and—proposition me in this insulting way.'

'The word is proposal,' Jago interrupted sardonically. 'A proposition has a totally different connotation, although you wouldn't know anything about that, my little Puritan. You froze me off so many times during our brief but eventful engagement that it was a miracle I didn't die from frostbite.'

'Oh, I see,' exclaimed Ashley, heavily sarcastic. 'Then it's all my fault. I should have allowed you to seduce me when you wanted to—and then this little local difficulty would never have happened.'

Jago pushed his plate away. 'Seduction,' he said levelly, 'was never what I had in mind. All I wanted from you, Ash, was a little human warmth—a sign, however fleeting, that when we were married, you'd welcome my arms round you—enjoy going to bed with me. All I got was one terrified hysterical rebuff after another. Is it any real wonder that my courage failed at the prospect of a bride who turned to stone every time I came near her?'

'And human warmth was presumably what the lady in the bar had to offer,' said Ashley, her heart beating harshly and discordantly.

His smile was twisted. 'No, it was slightly more than that. In fact, she made it quite clear that she fancied me rotten, and that was balm to my soul after having you fight me off night after night as if I was the Mad Rapist. I don't go in for one-night stands as a rule, but she caught me at a weak moment, and I was more than ready to enjoy what she was offering.' He paused. 'Now you know everything.'

'What a pity all I had to offer was Landons.' Ashley drank some coffee. 'And what a pity you wanted not just the cake, but the icing too. Getting control of the company eventually wasn't enough for you—you wanted passion as well. It never occurred to you that I might not feel particularly passionate towards a man who was using me only as a stepping stone to being chairman of the board.'

There was a silence. He said at last, 'Frankly, no, it never occurred to me.'

'You were clearly too used to finding your attractions irresistible,' she said savagely. 'And I was young and naïve, and easily conned, or so you thought. But I soon realised what the score was.'

'My congratulations on your perspicacity,' he said ironically. 'But if you expect me to bow my head and creep away in shame, you can think again. It alters nothing as far as I'm concerned. In fact, it almost makes things easier. You came to terms once with being married for Landons. Why not again? After all, you said only five minutes ago you'd give all you had to save Landons. Well, all I'm asking is our joint names on a marriage certificate—nothing more.'

Ashley laughed. 'You expect me to believe that?'

'Believe what you please,' he said curtly. 'But my little experiment at the Country Club last night told me loud and clear that nothing's changed between us, that you wouldn't countenance me as a lover at any price. Well, I can accept that. Three years ago

I tried to woo you into becoming my wife in the fullest sense of the word, and failed. So at least now we know where we stand. And didn't Silas always say his motto was "The end justifies the means"?'

'Yes,' she said huskily. 'He always used to say that. But I don't believe that any result could justify what you're proposing. Why are you doing this?'

'I've told you—I liked Silas, and I respected him and everything he was trying to do. If you hadn't turned up at the flat that night, we'd have got married and struggled along somehow for the sake of Landons. In fact, if I'd been around to take some of the pressure off him, Silas would probably still be here now, and don't think I haven't blamed myself for that. Perhaps this is my way of trying to make reparation.'

'But everyone will know why we're getting married ...' Even in her own ears, the protest sounded stock and feeble.

'What will they know?' he asked. 'They'll know that we had some kind of rift three years ago, and parted. And now, older and wiser, we're together again.' He gave her a wintry smile. 'Our tender embrace at the Country Club won't have gone unremarked, you can bet. Anyone remotely interested in our private affairs will take it for granted that our reconciliation began there and then.' He paused. 'When's the next board meeting?'

'On Thursday,' she said helplessly. 'But ...'

'Well, that gives us enough time if we apply for a special licence. We need to present the board with a *fait accompli*.'

'Wait,' Ashley said desperately. 'You're talking as if everything was settled—agreed between us, and it isn't.'

'But it will be,' he said. 'Think of it as a means to an end, Ash. You may not be able to stomach the thought of me as a husband, but I swear I'll give you nothing to complain of as a business partner.' He held out his hand. 'Shall we shake hands on a deal?'

Slowly and reluctantly, Ashley complied. 'There must be some other way,' she said, half to herself.

'If you're thinking of presenting them with Witham in my place, then forget it. He may be a wow in court, but he'd be out of his depth with Landons, and with you.'

She looked at him, her jaw dropping in shock as she registered his words, and realised that she had never even given Martin a second thought.

Instantly she rallied her defences. 'How easily you dismiss my personal happiness,' she began.

'Is it centred on Witham? You amaze me, darling. There must be more to him than meets the eye, if he's found the way to melt your icy little heart.'

'Because you failed,' she lashed back, 'it hardly means that no other man is capable of success. Even you can't be arrogant enough to believe that!'

Jago inclined his head politely. 'So it's only my touch that you find abhorrent. Well, we live and learn.' He glanced around him. 'This is a pretty flat. You should make a handsome profit when you sell it.'

'I have no intention of selling it.'

'Then you'd better form such an intention,' he said pleasantly. 'Your home will be with me at the Manor.'

'No!' she said hoarsely. 'I won't live with you ...'

'Now you're being absurd,' Jago said shortly. 'Our private arrangements are our own affair, but as far as the rest of the world is concerned, this is a normal marriage. And in normal marriages husbands and wives share the same roof. We are not going to be the exception. Do I make myself clear?'

'As crystal.' Ashley glared at him. 'Has it occurred to you that there'll be a third party sharing our roof as well, and that she may not welcome me at the Manor in any capacity?'

He shrugged. 'That's a bridge we'll cross when we come to it. Anyway, I don't anticipate that Erica will be at the Manor all that much. Giles left her comfortably provided for, and she's always had a yen to travel which he didn't share. There'll be nothing to stop her now.'

Ashley remembered the possessive hand clamped to his arm, and thought—nothing, except the fact she wants you for herself.

Aloud, she said, 'Erica and I have never been the best of friends. Perhaps I should mention that.'

He smiled faintly. 'No one's asking you to fall into each other's arms. I imagine you can manage being civil to each other for limited periods.'

'That,' Ashley said tautly, 'might depend on how limited the periods were.'

Jago frowned impatiently. 'Why look for snags?' he asked. 'Erica is my concern. I'll handle her.'

'Of course,' she said. 'And that will make everything all right.'

He sighed. 'Let's agree this isn't a situation either of us would choose,' he said. 'But the prime concern is to stop Landons being swallowed up by those sharks from Marshalls. Do you want to see your family's name used to dignify the kind of jerrybuilding they go in for?'

'No,' Ashley admitted in a low voice. 'But this—marriage you're foisting on us isn't going to be easy.'

He said flatly, 'Very little is in today's world. Don't worry, Ashley. If it becomes totally impossible, then we'll take the quickest way out. You're not being sentenced to life imprisonment with me.'

'I'm grateful for the reassurance,' she said tonelessly. But she didn't feel grateful as she began to gather the used crockery together. She felt frightened, and defeated, and out of her depth. The last three years of slowly and painfully becoming her own woman, of battling to control Landons, might never have happened. In Jago's presence, she seemed to revert to the bewildered girl, just out of childhood, and torn apart by her emotions.

Oh, it's not fair! she thought desperately, as she fumbled with a handful of cutlery. Why couldn't she practise the indifference to him she professed? And why, after all this time, was she still hurting, and hating him for what he'd done to her?

She ran hot water into the sink, and added detergent. Jago came to stand behind her. His nearness was disturbing, she thought, her body rigid as she registered the warmth of his breath on the back of her neck.

'So I'll make the necessary arrangements. We'll be married on Thursday morning, first thing, before the board meeting.'

'And divorced in the afternoon, after it,' she wanted to say. Instead she heard herself saying quietly, 'That would probably be best.'

She could still hardly believe what was happening. She was selling her life for the sake of Landons with no more emotion than if she'd been making a dental appointment.

'I'll be in touch,' he said. There was a pause, and she tensed, terrified that he was going to touch her—put his hands on her shoulders, and turn her to face him.

She couldn't face him. She was afraid he would read the confusion in her eyes, and she could afford no evidence of frailty where Jago was concerned.

After what seemed an eternity, she felt him move away, and a moment later she heard the decisive closing of the front door as he left.

Ashley found she was gripping the edge of the sink unit, her knuckles white with the strain. Slowly she unclenched her hands, making herself move away from the sink, and out of the kitchen into the living room, where she collapsed on the sofa, her body suddenly boneless.

She looked around at the pleasant room. Her home—her environment—her world, slowly and painfully put together from the pieces of the old one. Soon to be hers no longer.

She said aloud with fierce desperation. 'There must be some other way. There must be!'

Henry Brett's house was a pleasant red-brick villa with gardens sloping down to the bank of the river. As Ashley parked on the gravel sweep in front of the house, Shelagh Brett, who was bedding out plants in one of the borders, straightened and gave her a cheerful wave.

'Ashley dear, how nice!' she exclaimed, coming over to the car. 'Have you come for lunch?'

Ashley shook her head with a rueful smile. 'I don't think so, thanks, Shelagh. I don't seem to have much of an appetite.'

'Oh, this business with Marshalls,' Shelagh said with immediate sympathy. 'Such a worry for you! Henry was so sorry to interrupt your holiday, but he felt it was the only thing to do.'

'Henry was right.' Ashley looked about her. 'Is

he around? Could I have a quick word?'

'When last seen, he was tinkering with the mower,' Shelagh admitted with a wry grin. 'That thing spends more time in pieces than it ever does cutting the grass! But I suppose that's the nature of the beast.'

Henry was in the far garage, wielding a spanner, looking flushed and cross. 'Damned thing,' he was muttering.

'Darling,' his wife said, 'why don't you admit defeat and invest in a new one? Or would you miss these weekly battles?'

Henry got to his feet, wiping his hands on his ancient and disreputable trousers. 'Absolute nonsense,' he said flatly. 'The thing is perfectly good. I'll have it running properly in no time.'

Shelagh laughed. 'He's getting incredibly mean in his old age,' she teased. 'Do you think he's paid enough, Ashley?'

'Don't be ridiculous,' Henry said shortly. 'Let's have some coffee on the terrace.'

While Shelagh poured the coffee, Ashley made small talk, asking about their elder child Jeanne, now at university, and young Colin who was due to take A levels soon. She was genuinely interested. She'd always liked the Bretts. After her gipsy-like existence with Silas, their home had often seemed like a sanctuary to her, a place of total security. Shelagh was a serene and smiling woman, whose openly admitted priorities were her husband and children.

How nice, Ashley thought, as she sipped her coffee, to know such stability.

After a while the telephone rang, and Shelagh excused herself, saying it was probably a message for her about a forthcoming jumble sale.

Left alone with Henry, Ashley felt an awkward silence pressing down on her. She made a few commonplace remarks about the garden, while she searched for a suitable opening.

'What is it, my dear?' asked Henry at last. 'Has something happened?'

Ashley moistened her lips. 'You could say that,' she agreed carefully. 'I may have found a way of avoiding the Marshalls takeover.'

'Have you indeed?' said Henry, after a pause. 'Am I to know what it is?'

'Everyone's going to know eventually,' Ashley shrugged. 'It isn't the kind of thing you can keep secret.' She took a deep breath, 'Henry, I'm going to marry Jago Marrick.'

Henry sat up with a jerk, spilling some coffee. 'Damnation!' He mopped at the cushion on his chair. 'Ashley, this is no joking matter ...'

'I'm perfectly serious.' Ashley stared past him to the flicker of water beyond the smooth lawns. 'He—he came to see me this morning, quite early, and we—we talked the whole thing through. And I began to see it was the only way. As you said yourself, he's what the board want—a strong man at the top. If anyone can talk them round from recommending the Marshalls offer to the shareholders, then it has to be Jago.'

Henry looked in deep shock. 'Ashley,' he said faintly, 'you don't know what you're saying. People don't do things like this ...'

'Not in the normal course of events.' Ashley stared down at her hands, trying to imagine a gold ring on her wedding finger, and failing utterly. 'But saving Landons is the kind of situation which calls for extreme measures. I thought you'd understand.'

'Understand?' Henry almost exploded. 'For God's

sake, girl, you hate the man! I've seen your reaction each time his name has been mentioned. I don't know what he did to you—heaven knows I don't want to pry, but it was obvious to anyone that you'd finished with him for good. Why, even yesterday ...'

'I know, I know.' Ashley bit her lip. 'But at least this time I have no illusions to shatter. Our marriage is going to be—a means to an end. Nothing more.'

Henry was staring at her as if she'd just grown a second head. 'Child, no company on earth is worth that sort of sacrifice.' He made a clumsy gesture. 'We'll sort something out with Marshalls—insist on retaining some kind of control ...'

'No,' Ashley said steadily. 'Over my dead body. Jago and I have reached an agreement, and that will stand.'

Shelagh returned at that moment. 'Such a fuss about hiring a hall for a few hours!' She paused. 'Why is Henry spluttering? Has his coffee gone down the wrong way?'

Ashley shook her head. 'I've given him some unwelcome news.'

'You've made him redundant,' Shelagh said amiably. 'Perhaps we can get a new mower with the golden handshake.'

Ashley bit back an unwilling laugh. 'No, it's nothing like that. I simply came to tell him I was getting married, and he doesn't approve.'

Shelagh frowned at her husband. 'That's rather presumptuous of you, darling.' She turned to Ashley, her face anxious. 'Who's the lucky man, my dear? That young solicitor, I suppose.'

'If only it were!' Henry broke in thunderously. 'She's going to marry Jago Marrick.'

Shelagh's eyes widened. She said softly, 'Oh,

Ashley,' and took her hand in both of hers.

'Don't encourage her!' Henry almost howled. 'It's madness—sheer madness! Why, they haven't even spoken to each other for three years.'

Shaken, Ashley looked at him. 'I never thought you'd react like this,' she said. She tried to smile. 'Why, I even thought it might be you who'd given him my address and phone number. He must have got them from somewhere.'

'Not from me,' Henry said bleakly.

As Ashley put her coffee cup back on the tray, she caught sight of Shelagh's face, a mixture of guilt and embarrassment. She caught her breath.

'Shelagh, it was you, wasn't it?'

Henry sat bolt upright, staring at his wife. 'You?' He groaned in disbelief. 'Whatever possessed you to do such a thing?'

Shelagh sighed. 'Because he asked me, I suppose,' she said quietly. 'I wasn't going to tell you, Henry, because I knew you wouldn't approve. But I've never forgotten, Ashley, how much in love with him you were once. When you parted, and he went away, it was as if someone had switched off a light inside you.' She paused. 'Engagements are such difficult, edgy times. Sometimes people quarrel over quite trivial things, and each of them is too proud to make the first move. I never knew what had gone wrong between you, but when Jago telephoned me and asked how he could get in touch with you, it seemed like a new beginning for you both.' She squeezed Ashley's hand. 'And I was right, it seems. I'm so happy for you.'

'You had no damned right to interfere!' Henry almost roared, his faced flushed and furious. 'Why the hell did that fellow have to come back here now? I was afraid you'd do something idiotic—

that's why I was so reluctant to send for you.'

Ashley stared at him in bewilderment. She'd never seen Henry so upset before, and certainly never heard him shout at Shelagh.

'I'm sorry,' she said miserably. 'I didn't expect you to be delighted, but it seems all I've done is ruin your day. I'd better go.'

'I need a drink,' muttered Henry, and strode indoors.

Shelagh tried to smile. 'I apologise, Ashley. I don't know what's the matter with him. Worry, I suppose. I'll calm him down. He's been short with all of us recently.'

'I didn't realise he disliked Jago so much,' Ashley confessed.

'Neither did I.' Shelagh bit her lip. 'I'm sure he doesn't, Ashley. He was all in favour when you were engaged to him before. I think he's probably just concerned for you, that you're being hasty. He'll come round.'

'I hope so,' Ashley said quietly. She got to her feet. 'I'll see him at the office on Monday.' She paused. 'I'd like him to keep the news to himself for the time being.'

'Of course,' Shelagh acceded immediately, but her face still looked anxious as she waved Ashley off down the drive.

Ashley felt frankly disturbed as she drove back towards the town. She hadn't expected Henry's wholehearted approval for her decision, but she hadn't been prepared for such outright condemnation either. And yet she'd believed that Henry was as committed to the salvation of Landons as she was herself. That he would be as willing to grasp at any straw.

But his reaction had jolted her into a fuller

comprehension of what she was doing.

After Jago's departure, she had been almost in a daze, moving restlessly between one trivial chore and the next, until at last the once beloved flat seemed too claustrophobic to endure. The need to share her incredible secret with someone had been an impelling one. Now she wished she had said nothing.

She parked at the side of the road, and sat hugging herself, trying not to tremble, as she realised what she had committed herself to. How could she so easily have allowed herself to be talked into a fatal step like marriage, and to a man like Jago who had already demonstrated he was incapable of fidelity, or any decent feelings, for that matter? she reminded herself bitterly. And what hope could there be for any relationship based on sheer necessity on the one hand, and cold-blooded ambition on the other?

Jago enjoyed power. It was something she had recognised in him from the first, but it was familiar to her, because it was a quality he shared with Silas.

By agreeing to marry him, she had offered him absolute power, not merely over Landons, but over herself. He'd offered himself as her business partner, nothing more, but could it really be as simple as that? she asked herself desperately.

Could she bear to go on living under the same roof as Jago, day after lonely day, and night after sterile night, with nothing to look forward to except the possible, painful amputation of divorce to end the bleakness of their life together?

'No,' she breathed aloud. 'No, I can't. I can't!'

If her marriage was the only way to save Landons, then there was another candidate. Jago might have dismissed Martin, but he was a successful man in his own field. Why shouldn't the board find him acceptable? He might be new to the world of property development, but he could learn, as she'd done. And if she belonged to Martin, she would be safe from Jago for ever, she thought feverishly.

Exactly what it would mean to belong to Martin, she would not allow herself to dwell on too deeply. She liked him, and enjoyed his company, and wasn't that altogether a better basis for a permanent relationship than the delirium of joy and pain she'd known with Jago?

Martin's home was one of a small terrace of late Georgian red-brick houses. His car was parked outside, instead of in the lock-up garage he normally used, indicating that he was about to go out. Probably to see her, Ashley thought, bracing herself resolutely. He was a good man, trustworthy and reliable. The kind of husband most women would dream of, even if his first marriage had foundered. In one of his scant references to its failure, he had once said that his wife had found him dull, and resented the hours he'd spent trying to establish his career as a newly qualified solicitor.

As she stopped the car, the front door opened and Martin came down the steps to the pavement, carrying a small suitcase. He looked preoccupied, and Ashley called to him twice before attracting his attention. He came over to the car, forcing a smile.

'Ashley, I tried to ring, but there was no reply. I planned to write you a note. I have to go away for a few days—perhaps longer.'

Her heart sank. She got out of the car. 'Is something wrong?'

He said quietly, 'My—ex-wife telephoned. It's Claire, our little girl. She's been ill—measles, and there are complications. Apparently she's been asking for me.'

'I'm so sorry.' Ashley put a hand on his arm. 'Of course, you must go at once.'

'Yes,' he acknowledged unhappily. He roused himself and looked at her. 'I'm sorry, darling. I had all sorts of plans for this weekend, but I knew you'd understand. And it's nice to see you,' he added. 'You don't often come round here. Was there something special you wanted?'

'No.' She shook her head. 'I just—happened to be in the area, that's all.'

Martin kissed her briefly, his mind obviously elsewhere. 'I'll be in touch as soon as I get back,' he promised, and went over to his own car.

Ashley didn't wait to see him leave. Fate had taken a hand in her affairs, it seemed. Martin was no longer an escape route, but a harassed man driven by ties and responsibilities from the past. It was unfair and selfish even to attempt to burden him further.

She too had ties from the past, she could neither evade nor forget. Jago had come back, and she was in his hand, as helpless as a pawn.

But, between them, they could save Landons.

'That,' she told herself, 'is all that matters.' And wished with all her heart that she could believe it.

CHAPTER FOUR

IT was not, by any stretch of the imagination, the wedding Ashley had ever envisaged for herself.

They'd done their best with the room, Ashley thought detachedly, looking at the banked flowers, and the velvet-covered chairs in front of the registrar's desk, but it remained an office—a suitable place, she decided, for the enactment of the business agreement she had with Jago. She would have hated the hypocrisy of vows made in church.

There were flowers in her hands too, a charming arrangement of tiny orchids and white rosebuds which Jago had presented to her with an ironic glance at the beige suit which had been the first thing she'd taken from the wardrobe that morning.

What had he expected her to wear? The wild silk and organza in which she'd dreamed of enchanting him three years before?

She might not look like a bride, but she didn't feel like one either. She hadn't given herself time to think about what she was doing. She had gone to the office each day, dealt with correspondence, refused to issue any statement on the Marshalls takeover bid to the Press, and listened to Henry's daily pleas to her to think again.

'Disaster,' he'd said, running a hand through his hair, and making it stand up in unruly spikes. 'Sheer disaster, Ashley, I beg of you ...'

And she'd replied each time, from some frozen place deep within her, 'It's the only way. It's what

Silas would have wanted.'

She had seen Jago only fleetingly, to make the necessary arrangements for obtaining the licence. The rest of the time, she went to ground at the flat, which no longer seemed to belong to her. It was already on an agent's books, and potential buyers seemed to be lining up.

The furniture she had chosen with such loving care would be going to a saleroom. There was no place for it at the Manor. There was no place for her either, but she wouldn't allow herself to think about that.

She tried not to flinch when Jago took her hand and put his ring on her finger. The registrar was saying the final words, looking at them expectantly, waiting, she supposed, for Jago to kiss her. He bent his head, and she lifted her face obediently, feeling the brush of his lips like ice on her own.

She stole a glance at her husband, as he got into the car beside her for the drive to the board meeting, wondering at the cool confidence he exuded. This marriage was, after all, only the beginning. Now they had to win over the hard-headed businessmen waiting at Landons, persuade them to reject the Marshalls offer. The possibility of failure didn't seem to occur to him. She was the only one who was afraid, she realised, and not just of failure.

He looked magnificent, she was forced to acknowledge. His dark grey suit was superbly tailored, the silk shirt and discreetly sober tie equally immaculate. By contrast, she felt drab, but hadn't that been her intention?

The security guard's expression was curious when they arrived.

'Good morning, miss. The other board members

are here.'

She said a quiet, 'Thank you,' and walked to the lift, Jago at her shoulder. She did not look at him or speak as they rode up to the sixth floor.

As they walked down the corridor, Ashley could hear the murmur of voices from the boardroom, and squared her shoulders.

As they reached the doorway, Jago said softly, 'I think this is appropriate,' and took her hand in his, so that they entered together, united.

It was a long room, dominated by the portrait of Silas Landon which hung over an ornate fireplace. The fire was unlit, but the room felt close and oppressive as Ashley walked with Jago to the head of the table. She glimpsed the expressions on the faces of the other directors as they passed. She saw amazement, disbelief, the beginnings of comprehension, and in Henry's case, a kind of resigned despair.

She had prepared a little speech, and she delivered it with strained composure, telling them that Jago and she were married, and that she was resigning as chairman of the board in his favour.

An incredulous silence followed her words, then Clive Farnsworth spoke, offering a few stilted words of congratulation, in which the others joined more or less reluctantly. They were all clearly stunned, except Henry, who seemed sunk in gloom.

Jago was speaking now, his voice clear and incisive, but Ashley couldn't concentrate on what he was saying. Her gaze kept wandering to the massive portrait of her father.

She thought, I've done what you wanted, Daddy, but do you know the cost? Do I even know it myself?

It seemed to her that the harsh mouth was set in

lines of approbation. It was a scene Silas would have appreciated, she thought bitterly—the son-in-law he'd always wanted taking over the reins from the daughter he'd doubted. A wave of sudden desolation swept over her. She had made Landons her life. What did she have to take its place?

She was aware of a silence, and came out of her reverie with a slight start.

'Dreaming,' someone said with a chuckle.

They had always been wary of her in the past, but now there was a new indulgence in the air.

Clive Farnsworth said, 'We were just saying—er—Mrs Marrick— that you'll obviously have other matters than board meetings to occupy you today. There's not the slightest need for you to stay. No doubt there's going to be some hard talking.'

They were all standing, she realised, and someone was politely holding open the door. They wanted her to leave, she thought, stunned.

She said, 'But I'm still a member of the board.'

'No need to worry yourself about that today,' Angus Brent told her with heavy paternalism. 'I'm sure we'll all be happy to excuse you from any further part in the day's business. You can leave your proxy vote with your husband, naturally.'

'Naturally,' Ashley repeated with heavy irony. Inwardly, she was shaking with rage. She'd only stood down as chairman. That didn't reduce her to a cipher—someone of no account. She was still Silas' daughter.

She said icily, 'I prefer to remain and cast my own vote.'

There was an awkward murmur, silenced by Jago saying smoothly, 'Perhaps we could have a brief adjournment, gentlemen. Five minutes while I have a private word with my wife.'

Ashley watched them file out of the room. When the door had closed behind them, she turned on Jago furiously.

'What the hell's going on?'

He said calmly, 'You're an embarrassment, darling. Your presence inhibits them, and their wish to speak freely about the Marshalls offer. They'll find it easier to be honest—to say what's on their minds, if you leave.'

'You mean they want to criticise me—the way I've been running things since Silas died.' She was very pale.

Jago shrugged. 'I'm not a clairvoyant,' he said shortly. 'But it's possible.'

'I can take it.' Ashley lifted her chin proudly.

'I'm sure you could,' he said drily. 'But could they?'

She exclaimed passionately, 'You can't treat me like this! My God, Henry said they were hidebound, but I never thought ...'

'Henry was right.' He looked faintly amused. 'Don't take it so personally, sweetheart. This is your wedding day, after all. They can hardly be expected to know you'd rather spend it here, arguing about the company's future, than at home planning all the ways you're going to make me happy. They're trying to spare your blushes, Ash,' he added sardonically. 'Why don't you spare theirs, and go quietly?'

Her hand swept up involuntarily to strike at him, but he caught her wrist before any blow could land.

'You don't do that,' he said gently. 'Not now— not ever. Not unless you want me to reciprocate, and with interest. And I hardly think spanking you comes within the parameters we've set ourselves for our future relationship. Now stop being a damned nuisance, and let's play this particular meeting their way. When we've won, we can start re-thinking what role you're going to play in the set-up. But unless I do win, we may both end up out in the cold, and you won't help by alienating half the board by insisting on your rights as of now. Do I make myself clear?'

'You knew this would happen!' she accused, her voice trembling.

'I guessed it might,' he said coolly. 'As you'd have done, if you'd been as much on the ball as you like to think. In the same way, I'd probably have spotted the first signs of discontent long before Marshalls made their offer.'

'So wise, so all-seeing,' she snapped angrily. 'You know everything, don't you?'

He smiled a little. 'No. For example, I wouldn't have put any money on the certainty of you turning up at the registrar's office this morning.'

'What choice did I have?' Ashley shrugged, her green eyes sparking at him. 'After all, nothing matters except Landons.'

His mouth curled. 'If that's so, then why not allow me a free rein to save it? Well, are you going or staying? We can't keep them waiting much longer.'

She said, 'I'll go. But I won't forget this.'

'No,' said Jago, a muscle flickering in his jaw. 'Forgetting isn't much in your line, is it, sweetheart? Or forgiving either.' He took his car keys from his pocket and tossed them to her. 'I'll see you later at the Manor.'

'Where I wait, I suppose, like a dutiful wife,' she said bitterly.

'Yes,' he said. 'No matter how little appeal it may have for you.' He walked over to the door, and opened it, waiting with cold civility as she walked past him into the corridor.

The adjoining room was loud with talk, and thick with cigar smoke. Ashley walked past it without a second glance, aware of a sudden embarrassed lull in the conversation as she did so.

As she reached the lift, a voice, over-jovial and pitched slightly louder than the others, said, 'Sent her home to warm the bed, Jago?'

She didn't catch Jago's reply, but the burst of concerted laughter which greeted it made her smart all over as the lift gates closed on her, and it descended rapidly to the ground.

She was still hot with resentment when she drove up the Manor's curving drive. She parked in front of the house and got out of the car, looking uncertainly up at the imposing façade. Odd to think how she had once dreamed of living here. Now, every instinct she possessed screamed at her to take Jago's powerful car and drive it anywhere until the petrol and her nerve gave out.

But she couldn't do that. For the sake of Landons, she had to endure living here, somehow.

The front door opened, and the spare figure of Mrs Bolton, the housekeeper, appeared at the top of the shallow flight of steps, suggesting she was expected.

'Good morning, madam.' The woman's smile was vinegary. 'Mrs Marrick is waiting in the drawing room.'

'My cases——' Ashley began, but Mrs Bolton held out a hand for the car keys.

'That will be attended to, madam.' Her eyes slid sideways to give Ashley a swift head-to-toe scrutiny. She went on, 'I hope the arrangements are to your satisfaction. You'll appreciate that the notice Mr

Marrick gave us was extremely short.'

'I'm sure everything will be fine,' Ashley said neutrally. She had never cared for Mrs Bolton on her former visits to the Manor. She had been Erica's choice, she recalled, employed when Giles Marrick's old housekeeper finally retired.

As she walked down the hall towards the drawing room, the years seemed to fall away, and she was the nervous, uneasy girl she had been then, desperately seeking Jago and reassurance. It took all the courage she possessed to walk into the drawing room. She half expected to see Erica engaged on her everlasting needlework, but instead she was standing at the french windows, staring out at the gardens, and smoking with rapid, almost nervous movements.

She swung round as Ashley entered. She looked incredibly beautiful in an exquisitely cut grey skirt, and a matching silk shirt, her blonde hair swept with casual chic into a gleaming topknot. Her eyes, as they met Ashley's, were venomous.

She said, 'The happy bride.' She gave a small harsh laugh. 'My God, when Jago told me the news, I thought it was an extraordinary joke!' She stubbed the butt of her cigarette viciously into an ash tray. 'Are you quite mad? Didn't you learn your lesson three years ago?'

Ashley said, with a composure she was far from feeling, 'I learned everything I needed to know three years ago.'

'And you've still been fool enough to marry him!' Erica shook her head in disbelief. 'I wouldn't have credited you with a taste for blood sports. Or did you think Jago had forgiven or forgotten the way you threw him over last time? Because I can promise you that he hasn't. I could almost feel sorry for you.'

Ashley bit her lip. 'I prefer not to discuss my marriage ...'

'Marriage?' Erica interrupted stridently. 'What marriage? This time he isn't even pretending he cares a damn about you. He's got Landons, just as he always wanted, and he's had to take you with it. But when he's wrung the company dry, he'll throw it on the scrap heap, and you, Ashley dear, will be there with it. He's a cold-blooded, single-minded bastard, and he wants his revenge for being jilted so thoroughly three years ago. I don't envy you one little bit. Or did you think you were going to live happily ever after?'

She walked over to the sofa and picked up a jacket which matched her skirt, thrusting her arms into the sleeves. 'And now I'll be on my way, and leave you to enjoy your honeymoon in privacy—if enjoy is really the word I'm looking for.'

'You're going somewhere?' Ashley hid her relief.

'For a day or two. For the sake of appearances.' Erica's smile was catlike, calculating. 'But I'll be back. This is my home, after all. And believe me, dear, it's going to stay mine. No one wants you here. To Jago, you're just a necessary evil, so if you were hoping for anything else, you're due for a disappointment.'

'I'm not hoping for anything.' Ashley didn't even realise she had spoken the words aloud until she saw Erica's smile widen.

'How very wise! Keep remembering that, and you might just get out of this affair without too many broken bones. Although I expect Jago will keep you around for what's termed "a decent interval" at least.' She picked up her bag. 'We've waited for each other for a long time,' she added almost casually. 'A little more patience won't hurt either of us.' She walked to the door, then looked back. 'If you need some light reading for your wedding night, I should just check through the grounds for annulment. It's always best to be prepared, after all.'

Ashley listened to the fading click of her heels down the hall, heard her call something, presumably to Mrs Bolton, then registered the slamming of the door.

She groped her way forward as if she was struggling through fog, and sank down on the sofa, her legs shaking. She hadn't expected Erica to make her welcome, but she hadn't anticipated quite such blatant animosity either. So she hadn't misinterpreted the air of possession she'd noticed Erica exhibit towards Jago that night at the Country Club. Erica's tone of voice, her smile, had said louder than any words that she and Jago had been lovers while Giles Marrick was still alive, and it was only some mechanical observance of convention which was keeping them apart now.

She didn't even know why she should be surprised, but she was. In fact, she felt sick with shock, and an uncontrollable shiver ran through her.

'Your cases have been taken up, madam.' Mrs Bolton appeared in the doorway. 'Perhaps you'd like to see your room now. Lunch will be served at one. I hope you don't object to a cold collation.'

Ashley felt chilly enough. She rose to her feet, squaring her slender shoulders. 'I'm afraid I do object,' she said evenly. 'I've had nothing to eat this morning, and I'd prefer a hot meal of some kind—ham and eggs would be fine—served in about twenty minutes. And perhaps someone would light the fire in here.'

Mrs Bolton looked totally affronted. 'At this time of year, madam, the fire is never lit until the evening.'

'Never until now.' Ashley met the older woman's glance. 'Find me some matches, and I'll do it myself.'

Mrs Bolton's lips tightened until they almost disappeared. 'That won't be necessary, madam. I'll give the necessary instructions—and about luncheon.' She paused. 'May I suggest that you discuss any permanent changes you may be contemplating in the running of this house with Mrs Marrick—Mrs Marrick senior, that is. I mention it because—your husband gave orders that everything was to proceed as usual.'

'Perhaps it's a little premature to be talking about permanent changes,' Ashley said quietly. 'But when I do decide on something, you'll be the first to know.'

She saw shock in the other woman's face. 'And now perhaps you'll show me my room,' she added.

She'd never been upstairs at the Manor before. As she walked up the stairs behind Mrs Bolton, portraits of past generations of Marricks looked down on her—the interloper—with blank indifference.

The housekeeper opened a door, halfway along a corridor. 'Mr Marrick gave orders that this room should be prepared for you, madam.' She stood back, letting Ashley see the prim single bed. 'Perhaps you would confirm that his instructions were correct.'

It was her turn to triumph, Ashley thought, swallowing. 'Perfectly correct,' she responded coolly. 'I presume the door in the corner leads to a bathroom.'

'Yes, madam.' Mrs Bolton turned away. 'If you'll excuse me, I'll go and speak to Cook. Please ring the bell if you require anything.'

Left alone, Ashley looked wryly round her. It was like every other room she had occupied since childhood—well furnished, even luxurious, but strictly for sole occupation only.

Jago, she thought, had meant what he said, and it should have been relief, yet somehow it only served to heighten her sense of isolation. Erica's words rang in her ears: *'This time he isn't even pretending that he cares ...'* The muscles of her throat felt taut suddenly, and there was a burning sensation behind her eyelids. She fought the weakness back savagely. It had been an emotionally charged day, and it was bound to get to her sometime. But she wasn't going to cry. She hadn't allowed herself to shed a single tear on Jago Marrick's behalf since that night three years ago. She wasn't going to start now.

The afternoon passed with agonising slowness. Her meal, Ashley found, didn't help at all, but sat like a concrete wedge somewhere in her abdomen.

She sat in the drawing room, listening to the crackling of the burning logs in the hearth, and straining her ears for the sound of a returning car, or the telephone.

She was tempted more than once to call the office herself and see if anyone knew what was happening in the boardroom, but she thrust the temptation aside. Whether the news was good or bad, she would know soon enough. When Jago returned ...

She bit her lip, trying to quell her inner disquiet, as Erica's words came sidling back to torment her. But she had known what to expect, she told herself vehemently, trying to rally her spirits. The prospect

of sharing a roof with Jago might be a daunting
one, but it was no marriage she'd put her name and
hand to that day. It was a business arrangement, no
more, and when it had served its purpose, it would
end, and she would be free again, to live her life on
her own terms.

Free, she thought restlessly, adding another log
to the fire. Have I ever been that? First there was
Father, and then there was Landons. I've been
alone, but never really free.

She looked blankly down at the glint of the ring
on her otherwise bare hand. And now she was
more bound than ever.

When Mrs Bolton came to ask her rather
ostentatiously about her plans for dinner, she opted
for a tray in her bedroom. The housekeeper's face
showed no surprise at her choice. Clearly the
woman hadn't expected her to suggest an intimate
meal for two, to be served when her bridegroom
returned.

There was a selection of books in a small revolving
bookcase: classics, mixed with magazines and
periodicals on sporting matters and estate management, and a smattering of current bestsellers in
paperback, which were presumably Erica's choice.

Ashley picked out *Jane Eyre*. There was no
madwoman hidden in the attics at the Manor, but
its unfriendly atmosphere seemed to blend well with
the dour goings-on at Thornfield Hall. And Miss
Eyre's practical approach to her troubles suited her
mood.

She watched the early evening news on television,
then tried to take some interest in a wild-
life documentary, but found herself unable to
concentrate. The evening stretched bleakly ahead
of her.

I might as well go to bed, she thought.

Accordingly, when Mrs Bolton brought her dinner tray to her room, Ashley was already bathed, and in her nightdress and robe curled up in the one easy chair the room boasted, beside the small electric fire.

'Will there be anything else, madam?' Mrs Bolton drew up a table and set the tray upon it.

'No, thank you.' Ashley hesitated. 'That is—has Mr Marrick telephoned?'

Mrs Bolton's smile was edged with something that could have been malice. 'There has been no message at all, madam. Goodnight.'

Her solitary meal of soup, followed by lamb cutlets, completed, Ashley leaned back in the chair, allowing her feeling of quiet repletion to comfort her. Although why she should be in need of comfort, she wasn't too sure. She'd gone into this situation with her eyes upon, after all. The terms of the bargain were quite clear.

It was just that she hadn't expected to feel so—alone.

She'd never felt like it before, not even on that night three years before when she had wrenched Jago out of her heart, and, she had thought, her life for ever. Not even, heaven help her, when Silas died.

Tomorrow, she thought. Everything will be different tomorrow.

She shifted restlessly on her cushions, staring at the single glowing bar of the electric fire. But first there was this evening to get through, and this interminable waiting for the phone to ring, or the sound of the front door to tell her Jago had come back. She tried to read, but her attention, all her senses were attuned to his return, and she couldn't concentrate on the printed words which, after a while, began to swim in front of her eyes. Sighing irritably, she let the book drop to the floor and put her head back, closing her eyes. She was tired, she realised suddenly, worn out from the emotional turmoil and tension of the past week. And it wasn't over yet ...

She awoke suddenly to darkness. She sat up slowly, stretching cramped limbs, and swearing mildly under her breath. She'd only meant to rest, not actually fall asleep. The fire was still burning, providing the room's sole illumination. She pressed the switch of the lamp she had been using, but nothing happened. The bulb must have failed.

Wondering what the time was, she got to her feet and padded over to the door. Her hand on the other light switch, she hesitated for a moment, then turned the handle quietly and looked out into the silent corridor. Darkness there too, except for a thread of light showing under the door at the far end. Mrs Bolton had not described the layout of the house, but Ashley assumed it was the master bedroom.

And presumably, the master had returned.

Her feet made no sound on the thick carpet, as she moved towards the betraying light as if it was a beacon. Her knock on the door panels sounded startlingly loud in the quiet house.

There was no immediate response, and she was just about to turn away defeated, when the door was flung open and Jago confronted her. He had clearly been taking a shower, because he was wearing a robe, and towelling the excess moisture from his hair. His brows drew together when he saw her.

He said coolly, 'Is something the matter? It's late.'

'I know that.' Ashley swallowed. 'The—meeting must have gone on a long time.'

'Yes, it did.' The hooded hazel eyes, the enigmatic face gave nothing away. 'Perhaps we could discuss it tomorrow.'

'I want to discuss it now,' Ashley said sharply. 'Didn't it occur to you that I'd be waiting to hear?'

'It occurred to me.' His mouth curled. 'As the sole object of your concern, Landons must be very dear to you.'

'It is,' she said stonily. 'As I wasn't allowed to attend the meeting as I wished, the least you could have done is tell me what happened as soon as you got back.'

He lifted a shoulder. 'Your room was in darkness. If you'd woken and found me in your room, my motive might have been open to misinterpretation.'

'Not by me,' she said tersely. 'For God's sake tell me. Did they turn down the Marshalls offer?'

'Eventually,' he said. 'And—just. It was a bloody near thing.'

'Oh, thank heaven!' she whispered.

'I suppose that's a suitably abstract target for your gratitude,' Jago said harshly. 'A word of thanks to me would be to much to ask.'

She said stiffly, 'Naturally, I'm grateful.'

He smiled, not pleasantly. 'There's nothing natural about it, my sweet. But the fact remains, that however little you may relish it, you are beholden to me. I had to fight damned hard all along the line, and it's not over yet.'

'But you said they'd refused ...' Ashley began.

'So they did,' Jago agreed levelly. 'But I know Paul Hollings who's just taken over as Marshalls' managing director. We were at university together.

He's not a guy to give up the campaign, simply because he's lost the first battle. I suspect he has other weapons.'

'I don't understand.' She stared at him, biting her lip.

'Nor do I—completely.' He draped the damp towel round his shoulders, and gave her a look compounded from patience and boredom. 'However, I'd find comprehension easier, I'm sure, after a night's sleep.' He leaned towards her suddenly, the hazel eyes mocking and predatory. 'Unless you insist on staying and offering me some other form of relaxation.'

She jumped away like a scalded cat, and heard him laugh.

'I thought not.'

Ashley stared at him. 'You've been drinking,' she accused.

'Some of the board, anxious to assure me that they'd been against the Marshalls offer from the first, took me out for a small celebration, yes.'

'I see.' She gave a wild little laugh. 'I was here— shut up in this damned mausoleum, worrying myself sick—with never a word from you, and you were out—carousing!'

'Now that's a sweet old-fashioned word,' Jago said lightly, but his eyes had narrowed. 'But it was rather more inhibited than that my sweet. They were far too anxious to see me restored to the arms of my loving bride to turn it into a full-scale session. After providing me with a little Dutch courage first,' he added jeeringly. 'I think they felt I'd need it. How well they've got to know you!'

There was a sudden flare of colour in her face. She said angrily, 'They don't know me at all, and neither do you.' She turned, stumbling over the

hem of her robe a little, and went back to her
room.

She shut the door, and leaned against it for a
moment, trying to control her rapid breathing.

They'd won. This soulless bargain she'd made
with Jago had been justified after all. She should
have been jubilant. So why, suddenly, did she feel
so desolate?

I'm tired, she told herself quickly, that's all. She
untied the sash of her robe and slipped out of the
bulky thing, dropping if across a chair as she made
her way to the bed. The mattress was soft enough,
she discovered, as she slid under the covers, but the
sheets felt chill and unwelcoming, and she grimaced
slightly as she gingerly stretched out a foot, sending
a longing thought towards her electric blanket left
behind at the flat. She would fetch it tomorrow, she
thought. If she had to live in this house, she would
at least be comfortable in it.

But you don't have to live here, a small inner
voice reminded her. The company's safe. And your
marriage was an expedient which can now be
dispensed with.

Ashley twisted on her pillow, forcing it to
submission with a vicious thump of her fist. What
was it Erica Marrick had said—something about the
annulment? Prompted, she supposed, by the sleeping
arrangements Jago had ordered—the separate room,
this horrid, narrow little bed.

She sat up furiously, pushing her hair back from
her face.

I'm never going to sleep, she thought.

And, as if in response to her thought, the room
flooded with light.

For a moment she was dazzled, blinking involuntarily against the unexpected glare. Then, out of

the dazzle, came Jago, carrying, Ashley saw incredulously, a bottle and two glasses.

Open-mouthed, she stared at him. 'What—what are you doing?'

He seated himself on the edge of the bed. 'The fact that you'd been left out of the celebration seemed to upset you,' he said, almost casually. 'So I thought some champagne might be appropriate—particularly as this is our wedding night—nominally, at least.'

'I don't want any champagne,' she protested. She knew an overwhelming urge to grab the edge of the sheet and haul it up to her chin. He was too close, she thought frantically, aware that the hazel eyes were studying with open appreciation her slender shoulders, bare except for the straps of her nightgown, and moving downwards.

'Of course you do,' he said briskly. 'It's the best remedy in the world for the kind of incipient nervous breakdown you've been having this evening.' He smiled at her. 'Besides, you like champagne, Ash, or you always did.'

She was trembling inside. She remembered with an awful clarity the first time she'd drunk champagne with him. It was the night they had become engaged. Her father had produced the bottle, noisily insisting they drank a toast. Jago had lifted his glass in salute, his eyes smiling at her, and she'd thought her heart would burst with joy.

It was hammering now, but with a very different emotion.

'Perhaps I've changed,' she said curtly. 'Now, please get out of my room.'

'The room belongs to me,' he said. 'Like everything else in this house. My home, Ashley—not a mausoleum. Now, drink your wine.'

Silently she took the glass he handed to her, suppressing an urge to throw it at him. Silently she sipped at the pale, bubbling liquid, feeling its golden warmth caress her throat.

'That's better,' Jago approved, and topped up her glass.

'No more!' There was panic in her voice, and she hoped he hadn't heard it. It wasn't just the wine she was refusing, although it held an insidious danger all its own, but the whole situation with its enforced, unwelcome intimacy. It wasn't a large room, but the walls seemed to be narrowing, closing in on her, making her acutely aware of his physical nearness, oppressed by it. She wanted to move her legs, but knew, somehow, it was safer to keep perfectly still.

'Relax,' Jago advised mockingly, but his glance was searching. 'You're so tense you're about to fall apart!'

She said between her teeth, 'Is it really any wonder?'

'Bridal nerves?'

'Hardly,' snapped Ashley. She took another hasty swallow of champagne. Oh, why the hell hadn't she locked her door? she raged at herself. Or, better still, why hadn't she waited it out downstairs, where at least any encounter would have been conducted with them both fully dressed—where she would have been able to keep him at a safe distance.

'You don't feel like a bride?' he questioned silkily. 'But you should, Ashley. It's supposed to be a once-in-a-lifetime sensation, after all.'

'Not necessarily,' she returned sharply. 'When the company's problems have been finally settled, I intend to make a life for myself. It could include marriage.'

'You're already married, sweetheart—to me.' His voice was still smooth, but there was a note in it that triggered her defence mechanisms, warning her to tread carefully.

'Yes—well,' she said lamely, 'there's no real reason, all the same, for us to feel—tied in any way.'

'Why, darling,' his drawl was exaggerated, 'are you telling me there was no need for me to rush home to your side tonight?'

'None at all,' Ashley retorted, stung. 'You should have stayed in whatever bar you were drinking in. Who knows, you might have found yourself another willing lady.'

She saw a betraying muscle flicker in his jaw as her barb went home. 'Instead of which I came back to my unwilling wife,' he said quietly. 'Shall we talk about my reasons?'

'No.' Her mouth was dry. 'Jago, I'd like you to go—please,' she added with a trace of desperation.

'You told me you'd changed.' His face was an enigma. 'I'm intrigued. You certainly sound the same, Ashley—still as reluctant to have me anywhere near you.'

'I thought we'd already established that,' she said bitingly. 'Leave well alone, Jago. God knows, you've got what you wanted ...'

She stopped abruptly, the words choking in her throat as she absorbed the heated glitter in his eyes.

'How do you know what I want?' His voice was sombre, almost harsh. 'That's something I could never make you understand, but God help me, it hasn't stopped me wanting to try!'

He took the glass from her hand, spilling some of its contents on the quilt.

'No!' She sounded like a child, frightened and pleading, when she needed, more than ever, to sound like a woman in control of herself, and her destiny. But that control was splintering as Jago bent towards her, his face fierce with desire. Her little apprehensive cry was stifled at birth as his mouth took possession of hers.

There was no tenderness in him, she realised, just a raging hunger that demanded satisfaction. A satisfaction which her own physical starvation yearned to yield, to share. When he'd kissed her while they were dancing at the Club, she'd had to fight not to respond. Now, the temptation had doubled. The cool, clean smell of him seemed to be all she could breathe. The realisation that they were both next door to naked, the remembered weight of his body against hers, pressing her down into the bed—all these things were conspiring against her, undermining the sheer necessity of her resistance to him.

And the first wildness of that ravaging kiss was altering too, gentling almost magically, its violence being superseded by a warm and perilous subtlety. She could have gathered her forces to fight the anger in him, perhaps, but now it was an agony to remain passive as his lips and tongue caressed hers, coaxing a response with silken urgency.

Her hands hungered to lift to his shoulders, to hold him to her. She could have withstood anything but this slow ravishment of her senses, she thought dazedly.

When he lifted his head and looked down at her, she stared back at him, unable to speak, to voice her resistance. And perhaps something of her inner bewilderment showed in the wide green eyes, because for a moment his finger stroked the curve of her cheek in a gesture that was almost like reassurance.

There was no mistaking the expression in his own eyes. His gaze was burningly intense, heavy with need. The silence between them seemed to quiver, as Jago slid his thumbs under the fragile straps of her nightdress and slid them from her shoulders.

'I need to see you.' His husky voice was barely a whisper.

Ashley was trembling suddenly, remembering. This was one of the intimacies she had always shied from—his desire to look at her, to uncover her body for his intimate regard. No matter what persuasions Jago had used, what assurances he'd offered, she had invariably backed away as if she'd suddenly found herself teetering on the edge of some precipice. She knew, of course, that Jago was trying to coax her out of the shallows of passion into its deeper waters, yet it had never seemed possible to tell him she was already out of her depth and drowning in her feelings for him.

Now she was aware of all the old tensions, her hands lifting to cover her bare breasts, but this time he was too quick for her, capturing her wrists in his hands and anchoring them to the pillow on either side of her head.

Heated colour rose in her face, and she closed her eyes, her head threshing from side to side.

'Let go of me!'

'No,' he said quietly. 'Not this time, Ash.'

Her heart was hammering so hard, it felt bruised. Hammering so loudly, she could hear it.

Then, suddenly, she was free. Shocked, her eyes flew open, her lips parting on a little startled gasp as she clawed at the sheet, pulling it protectively across her nakedness.

And then she heard the hammering again. No physical manifestation on her part, but merely someone knocking at the bedroom door, she realised with a sense of utter absurdity.

Jago turned towards the door, his expression a mingling of impatience and disbelief.

'Yes?' His tone was not encouraging.

'It's the telephone, sir.' Mrs Bolton's voice was pitched a little higher than usual, but it was totally expressionless. 'Mrs Marrick—or Mrs Erica, I should say. She apologises for disturbing you but says it's important.'

Jago swore under his breath, pushing his dishevelled hair back from his forehead. He got up from the bed, tightening the sash of his robe.

'I'd better go,' he said half to himself, then glanced at Ashley, a wry smile curling his mouth. 'The lady picks her moments!'

Yes, Ashley thought. And she always will.

Aloud, she said, 'Please don't keep her waiting on my account.'

That checked him. He gave her a guarded look. 'Ash, listen to me ...'

'No,' Ashley managed, although her throat was strangling with pain. Only a moment ago, she thought dazedly, a moment ago he'd undermined her defences with his kisses so that she'd wanted to give him everything he could ask of her. But all Erica had to do , it seemed, was call ...

Humiliation burned in her. Hadn't she learned anything from that sharp, bitter lesson of three years ago?

She said, 'I've heard enough. I've asked you to leave. Perhaps now you'll go, and have the grace to stay out of this room in future.' She paused. 'I may be obliged to live under this roof, but it doesn't mean I have to put up with being—mauled by you!'

For a moment his face darkened, and she was terrified that she'd gone too far, then his mouth twisted sardonically.

'How inconsiderate of me to trespass on your maidenly preserves,' he said mockingly. 'I'd hoped the passage of time might have softened you, that under the ice and the resentment there might be a warm, living woman. How wrong can anyone be,' he added with a shrug.

Ashley lay watching, as he crossed the room and went out without a backward glance. As he'd walked away before, she reminded herself, then turned on to her face and lay like a stone.

CHAPTER FIVE

ASHLEY woke the next day with a headache—a sure sign that she hadn't slept properly, she told herself as she lifted herself up to one elbow to survey the morning. Although, in view of what had transpired the night before, it was a miracle she had slept at all.

Sunlight was spilling through a slight gap in the curtains, and frowning a little, she glanced at her watch. Then with a muffled yelp, she pushed away the covers.

It was late—terribly late, at least an hour and a half after her normal rising time. She'd neglected, she thought crossly, to tell Mrs Bolton what time she should be called, but surely the woman's common sense should have told her what office hours were like.

By the time she had showered and dressed, she was feeling slightly more human. The house was already busy when she arrived downstairs, and she returned the greeting of a woman in an overall polishing the furniture in the hall.

The dining room was empty, although the big table was set for one. Ashley checked, her brows snapping together. She turned and came face to face with Mrs Bolton, who had materialised silently from somewhere. Like some Demon Queen through a trapdoor, Ashley thought, stifling the annoyance that the woman seemed to provoke in her.

'Good morning, madam. May I get you

something?'

Ashley gestured at the table. 'I'd like some breakfast,' she said quietly. 'If you'd be good enough to lay another place.'

Mrs Bolton inclined her head. 'Certainly. You are expecting a guest?'

'Why, no.' Ashley was taken aback. 'I thought Mr Marrick would be having breakfast and ...'

Mrs Bolton permitted herself another of her vinegary smiles. 'Goodness me, no, madam! Mr Marrick had his breakfast and left for the day some time ago. He gave orders that you were to be allowed to sleep on.'

'I see,' Ashley managed, her hands curling into fists in the folds of her flared grey skirt.

And she did see, she thought furiously. It was bad enough being excluded from the board meeting yesterday in that high-handed way. God only knew what kind of a march he was stealing on her this morning. But certainly his decision to leave her resting hadn't been motivated by the simple milk of human kindness.

She said with all the calmness she could conjure up, 'Then perhaps I could have some toast and coffee. And make sure in future that I'm called at the same time as Mr Marrick,' she added. She glanced at her watch. 'I have a busy day ahead, I can't really afford such a late start.'

Mrs Bolton bowed her head in acquiescence, but her smile had a derisive tinge as she left the room, and Ashley had the feeling she hadn't been fooled for a minute.

She walked to the window and stood looking out at the sun-washed garden, her fingers drumming restlessly on the pane. I'm a cipher, she thought angrily. Jago has taken over my company, and

Erica still owns this house. I belong nowhere.

It was uncanny, but even Landons felt different. She was conscious of it as soon as she arrived. Conscious too of the stares and whispers that proclaimed her hasty marriage was the talk of the place. Or were they merely surprised to see the bride on the first morning of what was, ostensibly, her honeymoon? she wondered ironically.

She was glad to gain the sanctuary of the big office suite which Silas had always used, and she had inherited. She sank down into the high-backed padded leather chair behind the desk and closed her eyes for a minute. She had to forget about the events of the past twenty-four hours, she told herself, and revert to being Ashley Landon, girl executive. She had dictated letters before she left on Wednesday evening, and there had been no time to sign them since. She would do that first, then make a start on the figures the costing department had supplied for the Craigmore project.

She pressed the buzzer on her intercom. 'Bring in the letter file, please, Katie. I'll sign them while you dig out the Craigmore file for me.'

'Yes, Miss Land—I mean Mrs Marrick.' Katie's correction sounded flurried.

Ashley was tempted to say, 'Don't worry, it was an even bigger shock to me,' but she refrained.

When Katie came in with the letters, she looked uneasy, her usually bright smile muted. She stood watching nervously as Ashley skimmed through the neatly typed sheets, appending her signature to each in turn. And if she thought it was odd that she was still using her maiden name, she made no comment.

When Ashley had finished, she blurted out, 'Mrs Marrick, the Craigmore file—it's gone!'

'Gone?' Ashley replaced the cap on her fountain pen. 'Gone where?'

'To Mr Marrick's office, with the rest of the files. He had the security men up to move everything this morning. It was done before I arrived.' Katie shifted from one foot to another. 'I thought you knew.'

'I'd forgotten,' Ashley said calmly, after a pause. She even managed a smile. 'I've had rather a lot on my mind.' Her pulses were drumming madly. 'Which room did Mr Marrick decide to use in the end?'

'The empty one at the end of the passage,' Katie supplied eagerly. 'The one that used to be a store room. And he's got Sue Burton from the typing pool working for him.' She paused uncertainly. 'It's not a very nice office for him. Just a couple of desks and chairs, and the filing cabinets.' She hesitated again. 'I think Mr Farnsworth suggested he should use this room, but Mr Marrick said he didn't want to inconvenience you.'

Big of him! Ashley thought furiously.

She stood up. 'Fine, Katie. That will be all for now.'

When she was alone, she took a long incredulous look around her. The chairman's office, she thought, with its thick carpet and panelled walls, and enormous curving desk. All the trappings of power reduced in one stroke to a façade, a sham. Jago had taken control, and left her to rot in this big empty room.

'Over my dead body,' Ashley said grimly, and aloud. She got to her feet, thrusting her shaking hands into the pockets of her jacket, then marched out of her office and along the corridor. The door was shut, but she could hear the murmur of voices inside, and she opened the door and went in. Jago looked up from behind his desk with a thunderous frown.

'I thought I gave orders——' he began, then stopped. 'Ah, Ashley,' he said, getting to his feet with cool civility. 'I wasn't expecting to see you here today.'

'Weren't you?' Her smile was a brilliant, but her eyes sparked at him. 'Now where else should a working girl be but at work? Hullo, Sue.' She nodded at the secretary, who was obviously bewildered, notebook and pencil poised for further dictation.

Jago glanced at her. 'We'll resume presently, Sue,' he told her pleasantly. 'Perhaps you could rustle up some coffee for us.' When the door had closed behind the girl, he added drily, 'Sit down, Ashley, before you explode.'

'Don't tell me what to do, you bastard,' she said rapidly. 'What the hell do you mean by removing all the files from my suite?'

'Familiarising myself,' he said. 'With the company's current and future projects.'

'It didn't occur to you to ask me?'

'Frankly, no.' His voice was dry. 'I felt I'd probably had as much co-operation from you as I could expect—as last night proved.' The hazel eyes watched sardonically the faint tinge of colour that rose in her cheeks.

'That still doesn't justify your totally high-handed …'

'Oh, spare me the moral splutterings,' he said wearily. 'There was no easy way of doing it, Ashley, and Landons' problems are too pressing for me to tiptoe round your sensibilities any more than I have to. Yesterday you resigned as chairman, and I took your place. It wasn't a nominal appointment, and I intend to fulfil each and every one of my responsibilities.'

'Implying that I didn't?' Her voice shook.

'Implying nothing,' Jago said flatly. 'We've had this out already, Ashley. You did your best, but you were out of your depth from the start. Silas hadn't time, unfortunately, to teach you half the things you needed to know.'

'Such as?' she flung at him.

'Such as the kinds of things you can't find between the covers of a file.' Jago resumed his seat. He was in shirt sleeves, she'd already noticed, and now he put up a hand to tug irritably at the knot of his tie, dragging it loose. 'To know who, when and how to trust, for example.'

'Silas wasn't such a genius at that,' Ashley flashed. 'After all, he trusted you.'

Jago leaned back in his chair, looking at her speculatively. 'So he did,' he drawled. 'I suppose it's useless for me to suggest you do the same.'

'I discovered all over again last night how much I can trust you,' she said bitterly. 'You promised me that any marriage would only be a business arrangement.'

He inclined his head slightly. 'That's true—but did no one tell you, my sweet, that you can sometimes mix business with pleasure?'

'No pleasure for me, I assure you!'

'Unnecessary. You made your thoughts on the subject perfectly clear at the time.' His mouth twisted a little. 'However, it was our wedding night, and it would have been very unchivalrous for me not to have—tried, at least.'

She shrugged. 'If you have any other chivalrous impulses,' she said sarcastically, 'kindly strangle them at birth. And now I want my files back.'

He shook his head. 'No, Ashley. The files are

staying here. One of the reasons I chose this room was because it contains a very large safe—unused. You knew that? I thought not. A locksmith is coming this afternoon to change the combination. From today the files, especially those concerned with tenders, and projects still in the planning stage, will be stored in there.'

'My God,' she said slowly, 'the new broom really does intend to sweep clean.'

He smiled grimly. 'You'd better believe it. And from now on all files taken from this office will be signed for in a register which Sue will keep.'

'Oh—Sue,' she said derisively. 'May I congratulate you on your choice of secretary? If she wasn't blonde with good legs, she might still be in the typing pool.'

There was a silence, then Jago said wearily, 'Some of your remarks are beneath contempt, Ashley. I didn't "choose" Susan Burton in any sense. I simply asked the Personnel Manager to send up whichever girl was next in line for promotion. It turned out to be her, and I'm damned if I'm getting rid of her just to silence your waspish remarks.'

Ashley said sweetly, 'I'm sorry if I'm wronging you, Jago, but with your track record ...' She shrugged. 'And now if you'll show me this register, I'd like to sign out the Craigmore file.'

'I'm afraid not,' he said briefly. 'I'm using that myself.'

'But I was working on that!' She stared at him, aghast.

'You were,' he agreed. 'But it's a tender we badly need to win, Ashley, and I'm not at all happy with some of the figures.'

'My own thoughts exactly,' she said tautly, her

nails digging into the softness of her palms. 'And I'm quite capable of handling it.'

He opened a drawer in his desk and produced a sheaf of papers. 'Then perhaps you'd like to have a close look at these.'

She flicked through the sheets he handed her, her brows lifting. 'But these are finished with. They're all past tenders ...'

'Did Landons get the work?'

'No,' she admitted. 'But ...'

'But nothing.' His voice held finality. 'Look through them, Ashley, and find out why Landons lost. I'd like a written report.'

The silence between them stretched, quivering with tension. At last she said savagely, 'Yes—sir,' and lifted her hand in a parody of a salute. She looked round her. 'You seem rather cramped here, for someone of your ambitions. Are you quite sure you wouldn't prefer to take over the main suite, along with everything else?'

He gave her a level look. 'Thanks—but no, thanks. It may have suited Silas, but I find all that panelling rather oppressive—not my style.'

'I see,' she said wonderingly. 'And what exactly is your style, Jago?'

'You, my sweet, will be the first to find out.' He reached out and picked up the file in front of him. 'Now, if you wish to continue this cosy domestic chat, may I suggest you join me for lunch. Because now I'd like to get on with some work.'

Ashley was in the corridor, almost without realising she'd been dismissed.

Sue Burton was coming towards her, carrying a tray. 'Oh, Mrs Marrick, you're leaving.' She gestured at the cups she was carrying. 'I'm sorry I've been such a long time over the coffee. I'm still finding my way around on this floor.'

Ashley took hold of herself with an effort. 'It's all right,' she said. 'I—I'm not thirsty.' Not for coffee, anyway, she added silently. Blood, perhaps.

She went back to her office, shut the door, buzzed Katie and told her she was not to be disturbed for any reason, then burst into tears. She wept silently, her head bowed, and the tears scalding her pale face. Henry had warned her, but she hadn't listened. Erica had taunted her, but it had been too late. Jago, it seemed, had the reins in his hands and was bent on driving her down. Landons had the strong man at the top the company had wanted—but what place was there for her? He'd taken everying, and left her with nothing—treated her as if she was some junior clerk, as if the past two years counted for nothing.

But then they didn't, she thought. Jago's memory went back further than that. It hadn't pleased him to be jilted, and now he was taking his revenge by humiliating her in every possible way.

Her buzzer sounded, and she started. 'Er—yes?' At least her voice sounded steady enough.

'It's Mr Brett,' said Katie. 'I gave him your message but he wants to see you anyway.'

There was a pause, then Ashley said dully, 'Send him in.'

She had no secrets from Henry, she thought, as she dried her eyes. Or at least, not many.

He came in looking glum, an expression that sharpened to concern when he saw her.

'My dear child, what's happened?'

'Everything,' she said tightly. 'Go on, Henry. Say "I told you so". You're entitled.' She looked down at her hands, clenched together in her lap. 'I was too naïve to realise that when I resigned as chairman, I was also relinquishing every scrap of control I possessed in the company. I now know better.' She marshalled a smile. 'And I suppose it's the habit of new régimes to pile all the blame on to the old ones. Accordingly, I'm doing penance for my sins of omission with an office girl's job. Perhaps, if I'm very lucky, he may let me choose the next lot of plants for the reception area.'

Henry said heavily, 'I don't think anything will ever be the same again.' He paused. 'That was a marvellous performance he gave yesterday. You missed a treat. He's got the board eating out of his hand.'

She thought, And last night, he nearly had me ... Bitterly she said, 'Perhaps they'll turn on him in the end too.'

'Not if he comes up with the goods, they won't.' Henry roused himself. 'And that's what it's all about.'

'Yes,' she said tonelessly, 'I suppose it is.' She bit her lip. 'Did you want to talk to me about something special? If it's company business, perhaps you should go down the corridor.'

He smiled at her. 'It's social. Shelagh would like to invite you—and your husband—to dinner next week. She hoped Friday would be a suitable evening.'

'It's fine for me. I have nothing planned.' Ashley ran a finger along the graining of her desk. 'I'll mention it to Jago tonight at—the Manor.' She couldn't bring herself to say 'at home'.

'And there's one other thing.' Henry's face was rueful. 'I've been asked to mastermind your presence and his in the boardroom this afternoon at four.' He coughed. 'A couple of presentations. Wedding gifts from the board, and the office staff.'

Her face showed her dismay. 'Must I?'

'Oh, yes.' Henry nodded his head vigorously. 'In the eyes of the world, my dear, you're man and wife, whatever the private difficulties you may be undergoing.'

'Yes.' She swallowed. 'And he has put Marshalls to flight—as we wanted.'

'I suppose so.' He frowned a little.

You think they'll try again?' She remembered that Jago had hinted the same thing.

Henry hesitated. 'I don't think they're altogether prepared to take "no" for an answer,' he said guardedly. 'As a matter of fact, I was in Jago's office earlier this morning when the switchboard put a call through to him. It was from Paul Hollings, that new managing director at Marshalls that I was telling you about. Apparently, he and your husband know each other quite well.'

'So Jago told me,' Ashley confirmed.

'Did he?' Henry looked startled. 'Well, I suppose he has a great many business contacts, but I must say that this particular one—surprised me a little.'

Ashley smiled faintly. 'Oh, Jago is full of surprises,' she said with irony. Not all of them welcome, she added silently.

When Henry had gone, she pulled the sheaf of papers towards her with a grimace, and began to read through them. She remembered the first project very well. Landons had been invited to tender for the building of a new leisure centre and sports complex in a depressed inner city area. It was a prestige development, and the kind of scheme they were noted for, and they had been confident their tender would be accepted. Ashley frowned as she recalled the shock wave that had gone through the company when another firm had got the job, and

the continuing tremors when it had been discovered
to be a subsidiary of Marshalls.

In fact, all the tenders Jago had given her to
study had been lost to Marshalls, she realised, and
by a gallingly slender margin each time.

We didn't lose by much, she thought defensively.
No one can win all the time. We offered a
reasonable price, but Marshalls pipped us at the
post. These things happen.

She bit her lip. Yes, she argued silently, but
when the favourite for the race keeps coming
second, maybe there should be an enquiry. Perhaps
I should have called one—looked into the estimates
department, tried to find out where we were going
wrong.

With a sigh, she pulled a notepad towards her
and began to jot figures.

In spite of herself, she found she was becoming
interested in her tiresome task. When Sue Burton
phoned to say Jago was going to lunch and had
asked if she would join him, she refused quietly,
saying she way busy, and intended to grab a
sandwich at her desk.

Although she was not very hungry, she thought,
digging the point of her pencil into the paper. But
even if she had been, the sheer impersonality of
Jago's invitation would have robbed her of any
appetite she had.

As the time for the presentation approached, she
went into the small private washroom adjoining her
office and carefully and methodically removed all
signs of strain and grief. She kept a make-up kit
there as a standby, and she applied cosmetics
carefully, glad for once that they existed to hide
behind.

A nice mask, she decided judiciously when she'd

finished. And if her eyes were rather too bright, and if the smile on her lips had been painted there, she doubted whether anyone would notice.

Jago was waiting for her as she walked down the corridor towards the boardroom.

'Another act in the farce,' he observed sardonically, as he took her hand. 'Try and look as if the radiance was more than skin deep, Ashley.'

She glared at him, then schooled her features to pleasant anticipation as they entered the boardroom together to an outburst of applause.

Accepting the gifts was less of an ordeal than she expected. Ashley was able to unwrap the heavy silver tray from the members of the board, and the pretty china coffee service from the office staff, and exclaim with genuine pleasure while Jago made a speech of thanks, brief but humorous and drawing peals of delighted laughter from their audience.

'That was—kind of everyone,' Ashley said stiltedly when they were alone.

'And quick off the mark,' Jago agreed. He picked up the tray and studied it with a slight frown. 'Although, of course, this isn't the kind of thing you can pick up in a day.' He sent her a sardonic look. 'I imagine this has been waiting in a strongroom somewhere for just this auspicious occasion—probably for the last three years.'

She could think of nothing to say to that but, 'Oh.'

'I'll see these things get safely back to the house,' he went on. 'But I shan't be joining you for dinner tonight, although in the circumstances that's probably a relief. In fact, I shall be away most of the weekend.'

She stared at him. 'I see. May I know where you're going?'

HARLEQUIN DELIVERS FIRST-CLASS ROMANCE— DIRECT TO YOUR DOOR

Mail the Heart sticker on the postpaid order card today and you'll receive:

—**4 new Harlequin Presents novels—FREE**
—**a beautiful manicure set—FREE**
—**and a surprise mystery bonus—FREE**

But that's not all. You'll also get:

Money-Saving Home Delivery

When you subscribe to Harlequin Presents, the excitement, romance and faraway adventures of these novels can be yours for previewing in the convenience of your own home at less than retail prices. Every month we'll deliver 8 new books right to your door. If you decide to keep them, they'll be yours for only $1.99 each. That's 26¢ less per book than what you pay in stores. And there is no extra charge for shipping and handling!

Free Monthly Newsletter

It's the indispensable insider's look at our most popular writers and their upcoming novels. Now you can have a behind-the-scenes look at the fascinating world of Harlequin! It's an added bonus you'll look forward to every month!

Special Extras—FREE

Because our home subscribers are our most valued readers, we'll be sending you additional free gifts from time to time as a token of our appreciation.

OPEN YOUR MAILBOX TO A WORLD OF LOVE AND ROMANCE EACH MONTH. JUST COMPLETE, DETACH AND MAIL YOUR FREE OFFER CARD TODAY!

You'll love your beautiful manicure set—
an elegant and useful accessory, compact
enough to carry in your handbag. Its rich
burgundy case is a perfect expression of
your style and good taste—and it's yours
free with this offer!

FREE OFFER CARD

4 FREE BOOKS

**FREE MANICURE
SET**

**FREE MYSTERY
BONUS**

PLACE
HEART
STICKER
HERE

**MONEY-SAVING
HOME DELIVERY**

**FREE FACT-FILLED
NEWSLETTER**

**MORE SURPRISES
THROUGHOUT THE
YEAR—FREE**

✓ **YES!** Please send me four Harlequin Presents
novels, *free*, along with my free manicure set and
my free mystery gift, as explained on the opposite page.

108 CIP CAMP

NAME _____

ADDRESS_____ APT. _____

CITY _____ STATE _____

ZIP CODE _____

Terms and prices subject to change.
Offer limited to one per household and
not valid to present subscribers.

HARLEQUIN "NO-RISK" GUARANTEE
• There is no obligation to buy—the free books and gifts remain yours to keep.
• You pay the lowest price possible—and receive books before they're available
  in stores.
• You may end your subscription anytime—just let us know.

PRINTED IN U.S.A.

Remember! To receive your free books, manicure set and mystery gift, return the postpaid card below. But don't delay!

DETACH AND MAIL CARD TODAY.

If offer card has been removed, write to: Harlequin Reader Service, 901 Fuhrmann Blvd., P.O. Box 1394, Buffalo, NY 14240-1394

BUSINESS REPLY CARD

First Class   Permit No. 717   Buffalo, NY

Postage will be paid by addressee

Harlequin Reader Service
901 Fuhrmann Blvd.
P.O. Box 1394
Buffalo, NY 14240-9963

NO POSTAGE
NECESSARY
IF MAILED
IN THE
UNITED STATES

'I think that's my business, don't you?' he asked pleasantly. 'Although I'm flattered by your interest, naturally.'

She wanted to say, 'Are you going to be with Erica?' but she forced the words back. She would not degrade herself by asking, she thought painfully.

She said quietly, 'You're free to go where you please, of course. But won't people think it—odd, if we don't even make a pretence of spending some time together.'

His brows lifted. 'My dear Ashley, I wouldn't dream of asking you for such a sacrifice. And what people are you talking about, anyway? Mrs Bolton and the servants? I think they've probably drawn their own conclusions already.'

'Undoubtedly,' Ashley said grittily. 'But that doesn't mean I want to be dumped at the Manor, like another unwanted gift,' she added, stabbing a finger at the silver tray.

'And an unwrapped one at that,' Jago jeered softly, and colour washed her face.

'Don't,' she said unevenly. 'This—marriage was your idea, not mine, and I won't have it used to humiliate me.'

'Wouldn't it be more humiliating to have to play the part of the devoted wife all weekend?' he enquired satirically. 'I can't say I've been impressed by your acting powers so far.'

'I do my best,' she said coldly. 'But I won't spend the weekend alone in that hateful house.'

Jago's face darkened. 'There was a time when you loved the Manor,' he reminded her. 'You thought it the most beautiful house on earth, and you couldn't wait to live there.'

'I was a naïve child then, Jago. I didn't look below the surface and see things as they really were.' She lifted her chin. 'Not a mistake I intend to make again.'

'I'll go along with that,' he said coolly. 'Talking of looking below the surface, how did you get on with those tenders?'

I haven't finished going through them yet,' she said defensively.

'I didn't expect you would have,' he said. 'But you must have formed some kind of impression.'

She shrugged slightly. 'All right—I'd have said the figures we arrived at were the right ones.'

'So would I,' he agreed. 'Interesting, isn't it?'

'Frustrating,' Ashley said shortly. 'As we didn't win.'

'A temporary situation,' Jago said quietly. 'As I intend to ensure. I like to win, Ashley, and don't you ever forget it.'

'I'm not likely to,' she said tightly. She glanced at her watch. 'Well, I suppose I may as well go back to the house. There's nothing else to keep me here.'

He was silent for a moment, his glance almost wary as he looked at her. 'If the thought of your own company tonight is so intolerable, how do you fancy playing hostess?'

'Hostess?'

He said, 'I'm having dinner with Paul Hollings tonight. I'd planned to take him out somewhere, but I can always change my plans.'

'Paul Hollings,' she said slowly. 'The managing director of Marshalls?'

'The very same.' He watched her. 'It occurred to me that he might be the last man on earth you would ever want to meet. So when he suggested a rendezvous, I opted for neutral territory.'

'No need,' said Ashley. After her conviction that

Jago was spending the evening with Erica, Paul Hollings seemed very much the lesser of two evils. 'Invite him, by all means. After all, Silas always used to say it was as well to know one's enemy.'

'How true,' he said. 'As long as you know who your enemy is. I'll leave the arrangements for the evening to you, then. But bear in mind, darling, that you're a radiant bride. No shapeless suits or sludge colours tonight, please. Put on that dress you wore at the Country Club.'

She gasped in outrage. 'Are you implying that I don't know how to dress?'

'I think it's an instinct you prefer to suppress most of the time,' he said, the hazel eyes flicking wryly over her. 'No one looking at you today, for instance, would guess what a lovely body you're hiding under all that dull grey wool.'

She was blushing, she realised angrily. She said sharply, 'A compliment from an expert? Please don't expect me to be flattered.'

'I don't,' Jago said mildly. 'It wasn't really much of a compliment.' Amusement glinted under his eyelids. 'But then I haven't been allowed to look too closely, have I, my sweet?'

Ashley bit her lip. 'I can't believe that's a genuine hardship,' she said coolly. 'Be content with your other conquests, Jago. You won't add me to them.'

'Even though I've just warned you I like to win?' His voice was light, but it held an undernote which shivered across her nerve-endings. 'I lost out with you once, Ash. I don't intend it to happen again.' He paused tauntingly. 'Still want me around this weekend?'

Her mouth was dry, and she was trembling inside. He said he'd lost out, she thought wildly, but hadn't she lost too? Lost all the warmth, love and laughter her girlhood had promised—the anguish of his betrayal turning her to stone. Only stone could crumble, as she'd discovered to her cost the previous night.

Wasn't it safer, as common sense and reason were screaming at her, to back down and spend the weekend virtually alone?

She flung her head back and saw him watching her, his derisive smile anticipating her flustered retreat.

She heard herself say, 'I'm not worried,' and wished with all her heart that it was the truth.

CHAPTER SIX

SHE had plenty of time to panic as she got ready that evening. She had expected to be too busy to think too deeply, but the preparations for the dinner party were completely out of her hands. Unexpected guests at the last minute, she was given to understand, were no novelty at the Manor, and would be coped with.

Ashley was grateful to Mrs Bolton, but she wished all the same that all that grim efficiency could be swapped occasionally for a little human warmth.

After much heart-searching, she had decided to wear the emerald dress. She had little else that was suitable, she thought, reviewing her wardrobe, and if there were to be many dinner parties, she would have to buy some more clothes.

But at future dinner parties, she thought, Erica would have returned, and would expect to act as hostess. Ashley bit her lip. She would not be spending money on playing second fiddle.

But tonight she took her time, making sure her make-up was faultless, and her hair swinging in dark glossy wings almost to her shoulders. When her dress was on, she stood looking at herself in the mirror, composing herself, drawing her self-command about her like a cloak.

Jago was waiting in the drawing room when she went down, his foot tapping in restless impatience. The formality of his evening clothes added an edge to his already potent attraction, which took her by the throat, startling her. She threw her head back defensively, daring him to guess at the strange, secret flare of excitement, as his narrowed gaze travelled over her appraisingly. He gave a brusque nod.

'Thank you.' His voice was expressionless. There was a pause, then he said, 'Would you like a drink?'

'A dry sherry, please.' She sat down, smoothing the folds of her skirt. As he handed her the small glass, she asked, 'What's this Paul Hollings like?'

'When we were at university together, he had the reputation of being a go-getter. He's certainly come a long way in a short time.'

'You clearly have a great deal in common.' Ashley said acidly, as she sipped her drink.

Jago looked at her levelly. 'Perhaps. I thought it might be valuable to discover how much. Hence the invitation when he rang to say there were no hard feelings.'

'Do you believe that?'

'Hardly. I know what I'd feel in his place.' Jago drank some of his own whisky. 'It should make for an interesting evening.'

'And he's coming alone,' Ashley mused aloud. 'Isn't he married?'

'Divorced,' Jago said succinctly. 'I don't think settled domesticity was his scene.'

'He's hardly unique in that point of view.'

'Is that a dig?' He sat down beside her, making her acutely conscious of the proximity of his long muscular thigh to the silky green folds of her skirt. She had to restrain an impulse to shy away. 'What could be more domestic than this—my wife and I enjoying a drink together while waiting for our guest to arrive?'

She could think of all kinds of things, but she

compromised by remaining silent, and taking another sip of sherry. It occurred to her that Jago could sense her inner discomfort, and was amused by it.

It was almost a relief to hear the sound of the front doorbell, signalling Paul Hollings' arrival. Jago got to his feet in one slow, lithe movement, then reached down for Ashley's hand and pulled her up too, so that for one pulsating, tingling movement she was caught against him, breast to breast. Then, as suddenly, he let her go, and moved towards the opening drawing room door.

'So this is the enemy camp!' Paul Hollings was smiling wryly as he came in. He was a tall man, and very fair with the kind of good looks Ashley had always associated with Robert Redford. His hand gripped Jago's. 'It's been a long time, and after that stroke you pulled yesterday, I could wish it had been longer.' He turned to Ashley, his smile widening. 'Mrs Marrick, thank you for asking me to your home. Our companies may be rivals, but we, I hope, can be friends.'

'I hope so,' Ashley said politely, letting her hand remain neutrally within his firm grasp.

'I always knew it would take an exceptional girl to tempt Jago away from bachelorhood,' Paul Hollings went on, just as if he thought their hasty marriage had taken place for romantic reasons rather than expediency. 'Perhaps you could work the same kind of miracle for me, and find a woman who'd be prepared to put up with me. They all tell me it's time I tried again.'

'How brave of them,' Ashley said coolly, taking back her hand. He was as charming as all get out, but she wasn't fooled. He hadn't got to the top of a concern like Marshalls by exercising his charm. It fitted him as well as his elegant dinner jacket, but could, she thought, be as easily discarded. But she could do a line in charm herself, if required, and she smiled back at him now, turning on both batteries. 'I'll certainly see what I can do. Do you prefer blondes or brunettes?'

His expression didn't waver by a fraction, but she knew she'd disconcerted him. 'I'd say brunettes if Jago hadn't snapped up the most attractive one around. He seems to have all the luck these days. But mine may change,' he added casually.

'Perhaps,' Jago broke in levelly. 'Is it still whisky with ice?'

'Of course.' Paul watched Jago move away to fetch the drink, and turned back to Ashley. 'What a pity,' he said softly, 'that I didn't come to Landons myself to conduct the negotiations. You see, no one told me just how lovely you were.'

Ashley smiled at him, veiling her eyes demurely with her lashes. 'Do you really think it would have made any difference?'

'It might.' He looked at her mouth, then let his gaze travel deliberately downwards to the thrust of her breasts. 'You won't believe this, but my information was that you and Jago were yesterday's news.' He gave her a rueful look. 'I should have seen for myself, instead of letting him steal a march on me like this.' He shrugged. 'But it's only a temporary setback.'

It would have pleased her to fling the remaining sherry in her glass straight in his face, but she kept smiling. 'That we shall have to wait and see,' she said lightly. 'Here's your drink.'

The conversation changed to general topics, the two men swapping stories of mutual friends, but the little confrontation had unnerved Ashley. Paul Hollings must be very sure of his ground to show his hand so clearly, she thought uneasily.

Dinner was excellent, with sole fillets in a light creamy sauce following avocado vinaigrette, and preceding succulent duckling cooked in the English style with green peas and apple sauce. A pineapple shortcake completed the meal, and Paul Hollings laughingly declined cheese. It should have been a totally pleasant meal, but Ashley was unable to relax or enjoy her food. At this rate, she was due to emerge from her marriage with chronic indigestion, she thought with unwilling humour.

She excused herself from the table and went off to the drawing room, leaving the men alone to enjoy some port. She switched on the television, and flicked through the channels with the remote control device, trying to find something to catch her interest, and failing. She wondered what they were talking about. If it was business, perhaps she should have remained to hear what was being said. Jago might have moved her sideways in the company, but she would show him she was still a force to be reckoned with.

'You seem to be having grim thoughts,' Paul Hollings accused laughingly as he walked into the room. 'I hope they're not directed at me. It's just occurred to me that I'm intruding unforgivably on your honeymoon.'

'Well, please don't worry about it.' Ashley rose gracefully, and rang for coffee.

'Oh, but I do.' He sat down, giving her a long speculative look. 'If you were my bride, I wouldn't be sharing your company with anyone else.'

'Please don't play games,' Ashley said coldly. 'Don't pretend you don't know why Jago and I got married.'

He grinned. 'You're your father's own daughter,

Ashley Landon! I'm told he believed in plain speaking too.'

'That was certainly the impression he liked to give,' Ashley agreed coolly.

'Meaning I should look beneath the surface?' His brows rose questioningly. 'Is there any real need? I'd much rather have you as a colleague, Ashley, than an adversary.'

'I'm afraid that's too much to hope for.' She sent a restless glance towards the door. 'Where is my husband?'

'Making some kind of urgent phone call. He sent me to ensure you weren't feeling neglected.'

Or to make sure I wouldn't interrupt the phone call, Ashley thought with a hollow feeling.

She lifted one shoulder in a slight shrug. 'He's always so busy.'

'I shall have to see if I can't devise a way of giving him more leisure.' Paul Hollings' eyes glinted.

'I don't think he'd take very kindly to that,' she returned.

'Perhaps he wouldn't have a choice in the matter,' he came back at her smoothly. 'After all, your board is just delaying the inevitable, and our next offer won't be nearly so generous, believe me.'

She shrugged again. 'But as it's going to be refused, I hardly see that matters.'

'I wouldn't be too sure.' His voice sharpened, the velvet touch slipping a little. 'A company facing possible liquidation seeks any port in a storm.'

Ashley's heart missed a beat, but she laughed lightly. 'But Landons is nowhere near liquidation.'

'Not yet, perhaps, but these are early days.' The ruthlessness was overt now. 'How much work can you afford to lose to us, my dear? I know, even if you don't. Just think back on all the projects we've squeezed you out of lately, and we haven't even been trying.' He paused. 'I know, for instance, you're after the Craigmore contract. So are we, and we're going to get it. And that's just for starters.'

'So—war is declared.' She was glad to hear she sounded detached, and even faintly amused.

'It doesn't have to be war,' he said intently. 'We could call a truce right here and now. We could renew our offer, and you could recommend acceptance to your board. I'd see that neither you nor Jago would suffer financially. Isn't that a better proposition than watching your markets disappear from under your nose until Landons is worth peanuts? After all, we both know if you don't get the Craigmore development, you're going to have to start laying off some of your workforce. And that will be the beginning of the end.'

Ashley kept smiling, but her heart was hammering violently now. It was galling to know that Paul Hollings had a point. If Landons lost the Craigmore project, it would be a blow they could not afford.

She said, 'And just how long do you think you can go on undercutting us? It must be costing you too.'

'The margins aren't that great,' he reminded her. 'We regard it as an investment. Why don't you sell, Ashley, while you still have a commodity worth the name? Because I should warn you that you can't count on Jago's everlasting support, even if you are married to him. We go way back, Jago and I, and he likes to get his financial irons out of the fire in plenty of time. When he realises Landons is finished, you won't see him for dust. He gets bored very easily, especially with failure. If he can't win, he looks round for fresh pastures—but I'm sure this can't be any real secret to you.'

Her eyes flew to his, 'What do you mean?'

He looked faintly surprised. 'You were engaged to him once, weren't you? You must have discovered a few things about him.'

'A few,' said Ashley, recovering her cool with an effort. 'Of course, Jago doesn't allow anyone to know everything.'

Paul Hollings laughed. 'He must be a very complicated bridegroom!' He paused. 'Now, if you belonged to me, I'd want to share everything with you.'

She smiled gracefully, 'Perhaps I'm complicated too,' she said, as the door opened to admit Mrs Bolton with the coffee tray.

She was thankful to see Jago walk in behind her, but less than pleased to hear him say, as the housekeeper set down the tray, and turned to leave, 'Mrs Erica has left her ear-rings behind. Perhaps you could dig them out for me.'

So it had been Erica he'd been calling, she realised, pain striking at her. She reached hurriedly for the coffee pot, busying herself with the cups to cover the moment.

She had half expected Paul Hollings to raise the subject of the Marshalls takeover again, but to her surprise it was never mentioned. It was social chit-chat, touching lightly on economics and the political situation, without so much as a hint at the rivalry between the two companies.

Ashley contributed little to the conversation. Anger was uncoiling slowly inside her, tightening the muscles of her throat, curling her fingers into claws. And it had nothing to do with the fact that Jago was clearly planning to meet Erica during the next couple of days, she told herself vehemently. How could she possibly be disturbed by the confirmation of something she already knew? No, it was Paul Hollings' jibes that Jago might be prepared to sell out Landons, if the price was right, and run which were setting her on edge. That was the important issue—not some passing sexual infidelity.

Her mouth felt dry as she remembered that Erica had levelled the same kind of contemptuous taunt. Jago wanted his revenge, she'd said. '*But when he's wrung the company dry, he'll throw it on the scrapheap ...*' The words echoed and re-echoed in her mind. Could this be what had prompted Henry's warning too? Did they all know something of which she remained in naïve ignorance?

If it was true—oh God, if it was true ... Her fingers curled round the delicate porcelain cup as if she wanted to crush it to powder.

The pretty mantel clock struck the hour, and Paul Hollings got to his feet, smooth phrases of regret on his lips.

'I'm convinced I've thoroughly outstayed my welcome as it is,' he said, refusing Ashley's tight-lipped offer of a nightcap. He took her cold hand and lifted it to his lips. '*Au revoir*,' he added lightly. 'I'm sure we shall be meeting again very soon.'

Jago accompanied him out to his car. Ashley stood by the fireplace, drumming her fingers on the mantelshelf.

'May I clear the coffee things, madam?' Mrs Bolton had made one of her ghostlike appearances.

'Yes,' Ashley said abruptly, her mouth compressed, her eyes stormy.

The housekeeper sent her a sidelong glance. 'I hope everything was satisfactory, madam. Cook does prefer more notice if there are to be guests, of course.'

'I'll try and remember,' Ashley was aware of the curiosity in the other woman's eyes, and strove for a normal tone.

'Then if there's nothing else, I'll say goodnight.' Mrs Bolton's departure was as quiet as her arrival.

I suppose that's one of the things I don't like about her, Ashley thought. The way she seems to glide about the place, so that you never hear her coming. She'd make a wonderful spy.

She heard the front door slam and Jago's swift stride coming down the hall. He walked into the drawing room and closed the door behind him, his eyes speculative as he watched her.

He said softly, 'So—what's been burning you up for the past hour, or is it a secret?'

Her voice shook slightly. 'I don't like your friend.'

Jago shrugged. 'I didn't make it a requirement.' His eyes narrowed. 'What has he been saying to you?'

'Not very veiled threats of starving us of work until we're bankrupt, among other things.'

'Hm.' Jago came forward, putting up a hand to tug his black tie loose. 'I get the impression it's these "other things" which are really bothering you.'

She said, 'Can he do what he's threatening?'

If it was a plea for reassurance, it fell on stony ground. Jago's mouth twisted.

'It's possible. You know the way things have been going, or you do now I've alerted you to the fact,' he added with a trace of grimness.

'He's competing against us for the Craigmore tender.'

'Naturally,' Jago retorted crisply. 'I hope you didn't fall apart when he told you as you seem to be doing now.'

'I am not falling apart,' Ashley said between her teeth. 'Aren't you even a little bit disturbed by what I'm telling you?'

'It's hardly news.' His voice was clipped. 'Did he have anything else to say? I can't believe what you've been telling me could have provoked such a strong reaction from you.'

She moistened her lips with the tip of her tongue. 'He—he said if Landons went broke you'd walk away. Was he right about that?'

The look he sent her was compounded from irony and derision. 'Going down with a sinking ship may be very gallant, darling, but it makes no business sense at all. Does that answer your question?'

'Only too well.' She felt deathly tired suddenly. 'So much for your loyalty to Silas' memory which you said so much about!'

'But I'm also a realist.' The hazel eyes were hard and watchful as they rested on her pale face. 'However, the real trick is to prevent the ship from sinking in the first place. That's what we need to concentrate on. Or don't you agree?'

'You know my feelings,' she said sharply. 'Why else do you think I sold myself into this mockery of a marriage? I thought I'd bought your loyalty to Landons with the chairmanship of the board.' She gave a little harsh laugh. 'I'd forgotten, you see, that if you were for sale once, you could be so again.'

'Ah,' he said softly. There was a silence. 'Did Paul mention a figure?' he asked almost casually.

'He suggested the terms could be generous, for both of us.'

He smiled reflectively. 'He doesn't know you—does he, darling?'

'But he knows you,' she said. 'He said you "go

way back". Presumably he could be expected to know what you'd regard as your personal equivalent of thirty pieces of silver.'

His smile widened. 'He may have done, once, but my price has risen considerably since then. Well, aren't you going to ask me, darling? The million-dollar question?'

'If you don't really care about what happens to Landons,' she said slowly, 'why did you marry me?'

'To get you into bed,' he drawled insolently. 'Don't pretend you don't know. You've been as aware of it as you were three years ago, when you were driving me crazy with your touch-me-not tactics. I was prepared to be patient then, Ash, prepared to give you time to come to terms with your own sexuality, but I failed. You never turned to me, my sweet, never offered anything of your own accord. But you will, Ashley—that is if you want me to go on fighting for Landons for you. Because you won't win on your own—you know that. But I'm no knight in shining armour, darling. I'm a mercenary. If I'm to go on winning your battles, I want payment in kind.'

'You said it would just be an agreement,' she said hoarsely. 'My name on a marriage certificate ...'

He shrugged. 'I know what I said. I also mentioned something about the end justifying the means. Didn't it occur to you that can be interpreted in all kinds of ways?'

Ashley began desperately, 'Jago, I trusted you ...'

He shook his head, his mouth curling. 'I don't think so. You weren't really surprised when I showed up in your room last night. If we hadn't been interrupted, all the arguments would have been settled by now. Well, tonight no one's going to interrupt us, and you're going to start learning about what it means to be a woman—my woman.'

'I don't believe this!' Her dark hair swung violently as she flung back her head in defiance. 'You can't mean what you're saying!'

'I've never been more serious.'

In spite of her brave words, she knew he was speaking the truth. There was a cold purpose in the lean incisive face which terrified her.

She said huskily, 'And what about Erica? How will she feel, if she finds out? You don't really want me. You have a future with her. Are you going to jeopardise that?'

Jago shrugged. 'But she's not here, darling. And I certainly won't tell her—will you? Not that it would matter,' he added cynically. 'I'm sure, in her way, Erica has even fewer illusions about me than you. And if you're about to appeal to my sense of decency, forget it, because it doesn't exist.'

Her lips felt numb. 'Do I have no choice in this?'

'Certainly,' Jago said mockingly. 'Would you prefer to make love here on the floor or in bed?'

Ashley stared at him. 'You disgust me,' she whispered.

'Tell me something I don't already know.' He sounded almost bored. 'You're prevaricating, sweetheart, and I'm getting impatient. Well, shall it be here or ...'

'Upstairs.' Her voice was barely audible.

'Very well.' He walked to the door and opened it. He was smiling, but his hazel eyes were inexorable as they rested on her pale face and quivering lips. 'Shall we go up, then—darling?'

CHAPTER SEVEN

SHE went up the stairs ahead of him, her head held high, moving carefully so that she would not stumble. That, in some ridiculous way, was important.

When they reached her door she hesitated, but Jago put a hand under her arm and led her down the corridor to his own room.

The lamps on either side of the massive bed had been lit as though in invitation, she thought bitterly.

Jago said softly, 'Alone at last.'

'I hate you,' she burst out, and he nodded slowly.

'It's possible. My God, you must have had some motive for putting me through the torture of the damned three years ago! You left me with an ache in my guts, and now, willing or unwilling, you're going to ease that ache for me. You can start by taking that dress off—slowly.'

Ashley wrapped her arms round her body. 'You actually expect me to degrade myself ...'

'With Landons at stake?' he broke in softly. 'This is the price you have to pay, darling. You start learning to please me, and you start now. Unless you'd prefer me to undress you?' he added casually.

'No.' Her voice cracked.

'Then don't keep me waiting any longer,' he advised coolly, but with faint amusement dawning in his face. 'Don't look so stricken, Ashley. A lot of women make a good living taking their clothes off in front of complete strangers every day of their lives. They survive, and so will you. Or doesn't

Landons mean that much to you after all?' He paused. 'Shall I ring Paul tomorrow, and tell him that we've decided to recommend acceptance of his next offer to the board?'

'I'll see you in hell before that happens,' she said thickly. She reached for her zip, jerking it downwards, dragging with shaking hands at the fragile folds of her dress until it lay in a shimmering heap at her feet. She kicked it contemptuously away and faced him. 'Satisfied?'

'Far from it,' Jago returned drily. He beckoned. 'Come here.'

Her moment of rebellion was over. She went to him on reluctant feet.

She said huskily, not meeting his eyes, 'You've— humiliated me. Isn't that enough?'

It isn't even the beginning,' he told her flatly. 'I know all about humiliation, Ashley. Remember how you made me crawl on my knees to you?' His voice deepened in savage self-mimicry. 'Ashley darling, let me touch you. I won't hurt you, I swear. I won't do anything you don't want.' He laughed harshly. 'But it never made any difference, did it, you cruel little bitch? You enjoyed hearing me plead, loved turning the knife. Only now it's my turn. Before I'm through with you, I'm going to make you want me every bit as bloody badly as I ever wanted you, my reluctant wife.'

As he reached for her, she closed her eyes, shutting him out, but he ignored the tacit rejection, the long supple fingers stroking along the vulnerable line of her shoulders, and down to her taut, naked breasts.

Ashley stifled a gasp in her throat as his hands cupped her, the thumbs stroking in insolent torment across her nipples. She was rent by a sensation of pleasure so powerful it almost resembled pain, and it terrified her, demonstrating in one succinct lesson what she was capable of feeling, and more. And proving, she realised, that the wild, sensual cravings which had always so alarmed her were not dead, as she'd believed, but merely dormant, waiting for Jago's caress, as an early flower waits for spring sunlight.

Her whole body shivered, but in delight now as he touched her, and she had to sink her teeth into the inner softness of her lower lip to stop a little moan of acceptance and surrender rising in her throat.

The cool, clever hands slid down her body in a lingering voyage of exploration which seemed to miss no tumultuous pulse point, no clamouring nerve ending, hardly even checking as her last remaining covering joined her dress on the floor. Then the caressing fingers were on her spine, urging her towards him, making her aware with a shock of shamed excitement that he was still fully dressed, the brush of his clothing tauntingly abrasive against her total nakedness.

Slave girl mentality! she lashed herself in self-contempt. She flung her head back and looked into his face, her eyes sparking.

'Damn you,' she muttered out of her aching throat, and Jago laughed softly, and bent and put his lips against the jerking pulse below the smooth line of her jaw.

Against her skin, he said huskily, 'You take my breath away, Ashley. Now it's my turn to take ...'

He pulled back the covers on the bed, then lifted her fully into his arms and put her down on the yielding mattress, his eyes travelling with open hunger over every line and curve, from her rose-tipped breasts down to the shadowed mystery of her thighs.

As he turned away to shrug off his dinner jacket, Ashley flung herself on to her side, dragging her arm across her eyes, trying to shut out, along with the sight of him, the reality of what was happening to her.

She could always fight—make him take her by force, but a little shudder of recoil pulled her back from that particular brink. Besides, from the very first time Jago had ever taken her in his arms, she had been aware of the lean whipcord strength of his body, and the obvious restraint he had always practised towards her. Like a lion in a cage, she had thought then—only, now, the lion was free, and the risk of his anger was more than she dared kindle.

It was with her mind she had to oppose him, and her turbulent senses, with their traitorous clamour for fulfilment. When, at last, she felt the slight shift of the mattress under his weight, as he came to lie beside her, her mind dizzied into blankness and her nails clenched painfully into the palms of her hands.

He touched her bare shoulder, his questing fingers recognising the sheer rigidity of the delicate bones and muscles, and Ashley heard him sigh faintly.

He said quite gently. 'It seems you have another choice. You can either meet me halfway, or you can carry on being the virgin sacrifice. But I should warn you now, Ash, that I want you very badly, and I'm going to have you, whatever you choose to do.'

His grip tightened, making her turn towards him, forcing her to read the stark purpose in his unsmiling eyes. He took her hands in his, uncurling the taut

fingers, his brows snapping together as he saw the
little crimson weals scored into the soft flesh. He
drew a breath, then raised her hands, so that he
could touch the angry marks with his lips.

His voice husky, he said, 'Oh God, darling, let
go. Don't fight me. Don't make it be like this.'

'And how else can it be?' She hardly recognised
her own voice. 'You've broken faith with me, Jago,
over and over again. You can hardly expect me to
fall into your arms. Do what the hell you want—I
can't stop you. But for God's sake, get it over
with.'

He smiled slowly into her eyes. 'Is that what
you'd prefer? I'm sorry to have to disappoint you,
Ashley. I've waited a long time for this, and I
intend to enjoy every minute of it. You, of course,
must do as you please.'

He bent his head and put his mouth against hers
very lightly, his tongue stroking the soft outline of
her lips with tantalising gentleness. His hands were
gentle too, but very sure as he caressed her skin.
He knew exactly how and where to touch, to
arouse, to inflame to breathless longing, reminding
Ashley bitterly exactly how he had learned his
undoubted expertise.

It added steel to her resistance, turning dull
passivity to determination. She had endured his
betrayal and loss. Now, she would endure his
possession of her, somehow, combating her reeling
senses, and the wild urging of her awakening flesh.

But it was unfair, she screamed silently at the
warm, swirling universe of pleasure that threatened
to overwhelm her. It was unjust that she should be
so vulnerable, so totally at the mercy of her
responses. It would have been so much easier to
hate him if he'd been casual and uncaring—even

brutal. But, of course, Jago was none of these things. As he'd made clear, first in words, and now in this infinitely, exquisitely drawn out savouring of every quivering inch of her body with his mouth and hands, he wanted her entire capitulation, and nothing else would do.

Gradually, painfully, she retreated from him down some dark, emotional tunnel to a cold, secret place inside herself, where she existed in chill isolation. She made herself think—think about Paul Hollings and his threats—about the pages of facts and figures she'd studied earlier that day—about anything or anyone but the man in bed with her.

She succeeded well enough to achieve a kind of numb acceptance when, at last, Jago's body invaded hers in the ultimate intimacy. She had expected him to hurt her, had in a perverse way wanted pain so that she could turn the shrinking of her flesh back on him in guilt, but it didn't happen. He was too clever for that, too patient and too subtle.

Ashley knew a discomfort so fleeting it was over before she could clutch at it. She heard the soft, triumphant sound he made in his throat, felt his hands slide under her body, lifting her, locking her against him. He kissed her, his lips parting hers in passionate mastery, the thrust of his tongue against hers mirroring the increasing forceful demand of his loins.

He wasn't gentle any more. He was out of control at last, driven by a need so dark and desperate that all she could do was allow herself to be carried along by the storm of his desire for her. The culmination, when it came, was violent, his face wrenched, almost defenceless as he cried out, his body shuddering in release.

Then the taut body slumped against hers, his

relaxed weight pressing her down into the bed. He was the vulnerable one now, and it would be easy to push him away. But she didn't want to. In fact, all her instincts were clamouring at her to take the opposite course, to hold him close to her breasts, to smooth back the dishevelled sweat-dampened hair from his forehead, and touch his face with her lips. It was a reaction that startled her, horrified her, and it had to be dealt with.

She said icily, 'If you've finished with me, I'd like to go to the bathroom. I want a wash.'

She felt sudden tension grip him, and braced herself for his anger, but when he lifted his head and looked down at her there was nothing in his face but a faint, lazy amusement.

'To scour the taste and touch of me off you—out of you?' he asked mockingly. 'I wonder if it's as simple as that. As it is, the question's purely academic, because I haven't finished with you, my darling. Not by a long way.' His voice slowed to a drawl. 'If your lacklustre performance just now was supposed to turn me off, I'm afraid it hasn't worked. The night is young, and I have three sterile years to make up for.' His hand shaped her breast, stroking the delicate nipple until it peaked proudly under his caress.

He added softly, 'Starting now ...' and began to kiss her again.

Ashley awoke slowly and reluctantly, forcing her grudging eyelids to admit the instrusion of daylight.

For a moment she stared dazedly round, bewildered by the unfamiliar room, then memory came flooding back, and she sat up abruptly, eyes drowsy no longer, but alert and apprehensive.

But she was, it seemed, alone. She occupied the

rumpled bed in solitary splendour. She bit her lip
until she tasted blood as the events of the past night
came crowding back to torment her. In a series of
devastating lessons, Jago had taught her that he
had meant exactly what he'd said. He had made no
further attempt to woo her, but instead had used
her as if she was some instrument designed slowly
for his pleasure, and his enjoyment of her had
been unequivocal and totally uninhibited, she
remembered, a warm wave of colour washing over
her body.

And when, at last, he had fallen asleep, one arm
flung carelessly across her body, she had been left
to lie awake, shattered, aching with physical
frustration in every fibre of her being.

The victor with his spoils, she had thought
stormily, trying to fan the flames of her angry
resentment when all she really wanted to do was
burst into weary tears. But she had held them
rigidly back. The last thing she wanted was for him
to wake and find her crying.

She had won in her way. She had never by word
or gesture indicated that she found his lovemaking
anything more than a matter of total indifference to
her, crushing down her starving body's need for
appeasement. Yet now she felt utterly defeated.

She knew exactly what she could expect from
now on at her husband's hands. The question still
to be answered was—how could she bear it?

She pushed the covers away and swung her feet
to the floor, a glance at her watch showing her that
it was already mid-morning. She collected her
scattered clothes from the floor, then opened the
door cautiously, peeping round to make sure there
was no one in sight before running like a hare for
the seclusion of her own room.

As she waited for her bath to fill, she took stock of herself in the big mirror. She had escaped relatively unscathed. She had a few unfamiliar aches and pains, and some reddened patches on her breasts and thighs where the faint stubble on his jaw had grazed her, but apart from that she looked much the same, she told herself—if she didn't look too closely.

She bathed quickly, an apprehensive ear tuned all the time for sounds of movement in the bedroom which might signal Jago's return, then dressed, dragging on a pair of slim-fitting white cotton jeans, which she topped with a scarlet cotton T-shirt. She disguised the telltale fullness of her mouth with lipstick, but there was little she could do about the shadows under her eyes. But then it would probably give Jago's ego a fillip to have her going downstairs looking as if she'd taken part in some sexual marathon, she thought bitterly.

She took some of her anger out on her hair, brushing it until it shone, then started off downstairs.

There seemed to be no one about, although she could hear the whine of a vacuum cleaner in the distance. She hesitated at the foot of the stairs, wondering restlessly where Jago was. She must have been heavily asleep when he left the bed, because she hadn't been conscious of his departure. And if she was honest, she acknowledged, her face warming a little, she hadn't expected to find herself alone when she woke. He had awoken her more than once during that long night, his mouth warm and sensually insistent. Why hadn't he told her it was morning in the same way?

'Good morning, madam. Do you require breakfast now?'

Ashley spun round with a startled yelp, to find

Mrs Bolton had done her materialisation act yet again, and was standing at her shoulder, an unpleasantly avid look in her narrow eyes.

'Just some coffee please,' Ashley said, grabbing at her poise. 'And could you tell Mr Marrick I'd like to speak to him.'

She was allowed a glimpse of the vinegary smile. 'I'm afraid Mr Marrick has already left for the day, madam. He went immediately after breakfast. Did he not mention it to you?'

Ashley was very still suddenly. 'Oh, yes,' she said, after a pause. 'I—I'd forgotten.' She hesitated again. 'Did he remember to take those ear-rings with him?'

Oh, yes, madam.' The tone was respectful enough, but there was a covert, malicious glee peeping at Ashley from somewhere which was somehow more disturbing than open insolence would have been. 'I found them for him last night, as the matter seemed so urgent. Would you like me to bring your coffee to the drawing room for you?'

'Thank you,' Ashley managed as she turned away. Somehow, she found herself in the drawing room, stumbling across the thick carpet towards the french windows, flinging them open and drawing deep breaths of the cool spring air. It was a grey morning with a hint of rain in the air, and the dampness settled on her cheeks like soft tears.

She had not realised, she thought dazedly, that it was possible to suffer so much. She had promised herself she had wept for Jago for the last time. Now, suddenly, a whole new era of heartbreak had opened up in front of her.

Oh, no! she moaned silently, as pain tore into her, wrenching her apart. How could this be happening? How could Jago, the faithless, the opportunist, still have the power to hurt her like this?

And she heard the desperate truth ringing through her heart, soul and mind.

'Because I love him, God help me. I still love him.'

She stood for what seemed like an eternity, staring across the windless garden with eyes that saw nothing.

She wondered how she could have been such a fool not to recognise the conflict inside her for what it was—and thought what irony it was that recognition should have come at this moment, when it had just been brought home to her, yet again, that she had nothing to hope for in any relationship with him. Last night he had possessed her body, claiming that last remaining asset Landons had brought him, she thought bitterly, and that was all it had meant to him. His cynical absence this morning proved that.

Pride told her that she should be glad she had resisted the potent sensual magic of his lovemaking, giving nothing in return, making him take. Because if she had surrendered, given way to the urgency within her, it would have made no difference. She would still have woken—alone.

She couldn't even be jealous of Erica, because she knew that Jago would never truly belong to her either, no matter how passionate their affair. He had his own priorities, and any woman in his life would have to accustom herself to occupying a place somewhere down on the list. Even Erica.

For herself, she was thankful Jago couldn't know, and wouldn't ever know about the bruised, vulnerable confusion inside her. Loving him was her grief, and had to remain her secret.

Shivering, she turned back into the drawing room, as Mrs Bolton arrived with the coffee tray.

Ashley said, 'I see the fire hasn't been lit again.'

'Mrs Marrick's orders, madam, are ...'

'I am Mrs Marrick.' Ashley's voice was cool and sharp. 'And while this cool weather continues, I require the drawing room fire to be lit each morning. Do I make myself clear?'

'Perfectly clear.' Mrs Bolton's meagre bosom swelled. 'But I am used to taking my orders from Mrs Erica. And I should point out—madam, that she will not be pleased to find her instructions being countermanded.'

'And nor am I,' Ashley said quietly. 'I think you and I are going to have to come to terms, Mrs Bolton, or else a parting of the ways.'

A mottled flush appeared on Mrs Bolton's face and neck. 'You have no right ...'

'I think you'll find I have.' Ashley poured herself some coffee. 'Shall we say a month's notice?'

'You can say what you please!' The older woman was making no effort to conceal her contempt now. 'It will make no difference, as you'll find out. We'll just see which of us is the one who's leaving!'

The drawing room closed behind her with a slam.

Phew! thought Ashley, leaning back in her chair. The confrontation seemed to have blown up out of nowhere, but it had been inevitable. She remembered her first shy visits to the Manor as Jago's fiancée three years before, and how gauche and schoolgirlish Mrs Bolton had managed to make her feel. But not again, she told herself grimly. Mrs Bolton was a born bully, homing in on weakness wherever she saw it, but Ashley was no longer the child she had been. Her mouth twisted. If nothing else, Jago had seen to that.

And for a while, for better or worse, the Manor was to be her home.

She gave her surroundings a wry look. They might be elegant, but they were far from homelike. The drawing room alone looked like an illustration from an upmarket furnishing magazine, but it was not cosy in any way. The only really comfortable room, she recalled, had been Giles Marrick's study, which he had kept jealously to himself, and which Jago now used. Perhaps she too would adopt a room, and make it her own.

Because there was no denying the Manor lacked heart. She supposed that was what happened to a house like this when it lacked the children, and the pets, and the sprawling family life it had been originally intended for.

Ashley swallowed past a painful lump her throat. Well, there was nothing she could do about that, but she could organise her own room. She knew where to go too.

There was a small morning room at the rear of the house, overlooking the shrubbery. It was dark, and rather cramped, and probably for that reason it had escaped the glossy patina which Erica had imposed on the rest of the house.

The furniture was heavy and old-fashioned, and needed relegating to an attic, she decided critically. She could easily replace it with some of the favourite pieces from her flat. She would keep the faded charm of the silk wallpaper, however, but add lighter curtains. And she would start now.

Taking a deep breath, she summoned Mrs Bolton and told her quietly that she wanted the room cleared. She had expected further protests, but apart from the inevitable tightening of the lips, Mrs Bolton showed no sign of dissent.

She probably thinks a small back room is the best place for me, Ashley decided with faint amusement.

She drove into town. The estate agent was not altogether pleased when she told him she had changed her mind about selling all her furniture, although he admitted reluctantly that he hadn't cleared the flat yet.

And he was pardonably annoyed when she said she was no longer interested in selling the flat, but letting it part furnished instead. It seemed he had two clients involved in a contract race already.

Ashley shrugged. 'Ask if they're interested in a short-term lease instead.'

'They won't be,' he said mournfully. 'May I know why you've changed your mind? Mr Marrick was quite positive that you wanted to sell.'

She caught a speculative gleam in his eye, and smiled nonchalantly. 'We talked it over, and decided a *pied-à-terre* near the office might not be such a bad thing to hang on to.'

It was odd, letting herself back into the flat again. It had only been a few days since she had left it, yet it seemed like a lifetime. And it was a desirable property, she thought as she wandered through the rooms. It was no wonder it had been so easy to dispose of. What she hadn't bargained for was feeling a stranger in her own home, and she didn't like it.

'Hey!' she said aloud, looking around her. 'I haven't been away that long. And I'm going to need you to come back to, so don't you reject me.'

She decided on the furniture she would have at the Manor, and tagged and labelled it. The agent had given her the phone number of a reliable firm which did small removals, and she was dialling them when she heard someone at the front door. Another interested client, she thought, as she opened it.

'Martin!' She couldn't have been more taken aback.

He looked in a state of shock himself. 'Someone said the flat was up for sale and then they told me ...' He stopped abruptly. 'Ashley, it can't be true! You're not—married?'

Mutely, she extended her left hand.

'Good God!' He leaned weakly against the door jamb. 'You don't waste any time, do you? I mean, when I went away, I thought—I intended ...' He stopped again. 'You must have known.'

She felt sorry to her soul. But there was no way she could tell him that, in spite of his intentions, their relationship would always have been fruitless. Because, in her secret heart, she had always been waiting for Jago to come back. She couldn't damage Martin's pride by even hinting at that.

She said awkwardly, 'Would you like a drink? There's still some here. I can't offer you coffee because the power's turned off.'

'I could do with something,' he muttered.

Ashley let him in reluctantly, and busied herself finding the remains of the whisky, and two glasses. She poured him a measure of Scotch, and filled her own glass with bitter lemon.

She said too brightly, 'How's your little girl? Better?'

'Yes—oh, yes. Children shake these things off so quickly. And my—Susan was always prone to panic rather.' There was a wistfulness in his voice. Martin missed being married, she thought sadly. He missed being masterful and reassuring. Only those weren't the qualities she'd been looking for. Unknown to herself, she liked living dangerously, she thought wretchedly.

He said, 'Of course, I wondered when I saw you and Marrick together at the Country Club. But you were so positive that it was all over. I thought I could trust you.'

His tone irritated her. She said, 'I didn't think we'd reached that degree of exclusivity. I'm sorry.'

Martin stirred restively. 'There are all kinds of rumours flying around. I suppose you know that.'

She shrugged, and sipped her drink. 'Inevitable, I suppose. Under the circumstances.'

'What are the circumstances?' The note of injury was more pronounced. 'I think I have a right to ask.'

'And I have an equal right to keep silent,' she said gently. 'Martin, don't push.'

There was a lengthy silence, then he sighed. 'I'm sorry. But you might have let me know what the situation was, instead of letting me come back here, thinking that everything between us was fine. That we'd be taking up where we left off.'

'It was thoughtless,' she agreed. 'Let's just say Jago—swept me off my feet, and leave it at that, shall we?'

'Perhaps I should have tried that,' he said ruefully. He finished his whisky and got to this feet. 'Well, no hard feelings, Ashley. Am I allowed to kiss you goodbye?'

The short answer to that was 'No', but she didn't want to injure his feelings any further, so when he took her arms and drew her towards him, she went passively, lifting closed lips to his touch. Only Martin didn't see it that way at all. His mouth fastened on hers greedily, sucking and tugging, while his tongue tried insistently to force an entry. Her hands came up and pushed at his chest with sufficient force to let him know this wasn't mere coyness. But he was in no hurry to let go, she realised with mingled dismay and annoyance. He was set on proving his point, making his mark—showing her that it could have worked for them. And all she could feel in return was a muted remorse.

As his hands slid down her arms to touch her breasts, Ashley stiffened. The situation was getting out of control, and it was going to take one shrewd, upward jerk of her knee to bring him to his senses.

And as she nerved herself to do it, a voice from the doorway said with a bite like an arctic wind, 'I seem to have arrived at a bad moment.'

It was Jago.

CHAPTER EIGHT

MARTIN let her go so suddenly, she nearly fell over. His face was so nonplussed as to be almost comic. He'd clearly remembered that this was an important client's wife he'd just been caught embracing. Ashley could have burst into hysterical laughter, only it wasn't funny. It wasn't funny at all.

He said, stumbling over his words, 'I—I ought to explain ...'

The sardonic expression on Jago's face riled Ashley. What right had he to put Martin through any kind of hoop, she asked herself stormily. Or did he think there was one law for him, and a different one for everyone else?

She said swiftly, 'There's no need, Martin. Goodbye, and good luck.'

'Good luck, indeed,' Jago said silkily, as Martin sidled past him. 'I presume you can find your own way out.'

Husband and wife waited in silence for the sound of the front door closing behind him, then Jago said, 'I suppose I should apologise for my intrusion. But I'm not going to.' The hazel eyes were harsh. 'I wondered what the hell was going on when Jack Macauley phoned, bleating about you taking this place off the market. I didn't realise you were planning to turn it into a love nest.'

'I'm not,' Ashley said tightly. 'Martin was just—saying goodbye.'

'Oh, really?' There was an insolent challenge in

his voice. 'It looked more like hello to me.'

The colour in her face deepened hectically. 'Don't be sarcastic!' she snapped.

Jago shrugged. 'Didn't last night warn you what to expect?'

She didn't know what to say in answer to that, so she picked up the used glasses and took them to the kitchen, rinsing them under the cold tap.

Jago followed her. She was all too conscious of him watching her as she busied herself at the sink.

She said resentfully, 'How did you know I'd be here?'

'Your car was outside,' he said. 'You're not very good at the assignation game, are you, Ash? You should park several streets away, and walk if you don't want to be caught.'

'Thanks for the expert advice. I'll try and remember.' She tried to match the satire in his voice.

'So why have you decided to let instead of sell? And why are the gardeners at the Manor indoors, heaving furniture all over the place?'

It was Ashley's turn to shrug. 'I decided to take over the morning room for my own use. No one seems to want it, and I would like some privacy, and my own things about me.' She paused. 'I hope you don't object.'

'In the daytime, you can do as you please,' Jago said. 'But the nights are different, and I've given some orders of my own about those. Your clothes and belongings are being moved to my bedroom.'

'Oh.' She could feel herself flushing again, and kept her back rigidly turned. 'Was that necessary?'

'Yes,' he said. 'Or did you think last night was all there was to it?'

'I've tried not to think about it at all.'

He gave a short laugh. 'I can believe that.' He paused. 'So—why are you keeping a stake in this place?'

'So that I'll have somewhere to go,' she said evenly. 'When you get tired of all these little power games of yours, and decide to let me go, that is.'

'Is that what I'm planning?' He sounded amused.

'God knows,' she said shortly. 'But I'm not letting the flat go. If Macauleys can't find me any short-term tenants, then the place can stay empty. I presume I'm still going to be paid some kind of salary from Landons, so that I can keep the mortgage payments going.'

'Of course. As long as you don't make a habit of using the place to entertain other men.'

She turned then, to face him, angry and at bay. 'You hypocrite! Do you think for one moment I don't know where you've been this morning?'

'I imagine you do. I didn't intend to make a secret of it.'

'An open marriage, in other words. Please don't forget that can work both ways.'

'I shan't,' said Jago, after a pause. 'Although your reaction last night didn't prompt me to suppose you were planning to fling yourself headlong into the sexual deeps.'

Ashley jerked a shoulder. She said clearly, 'Just because you don't turn me on ...'

Her voice trailed away into a charged silence. 'I see,' Jago said at last. 'So it's—anyone's kisses but mine. Is that it?'

'Perhaps,' she said. She didn't look at him. 'Now, I'd better phone that removal firm.'

'Later,' Jago said too gently. 'After all, they might remove the bed, and I have a use for it.'

As he moved towards her, Ashley read the

purpose in his eyes with real alarm. She would have retreated, but she was pinned against the sink, with nowhere to go.

She said shakily, 'You're being ridiculous ...'

'Probably,' he said. 'But what the hell! After all, I spoiled your little rendezvous with Witham, so the least I can do is make it up to you for that.'

'I hadn't planned to meet him,' she protested. 'He'd been away. He came round to see me because he'd just heard the news ...'

'Of course he did.' He took her by the shoulders, drawing her towards him, the hazel eyes hard and mocking as they studied her flushed, pleading face. 'And then I turned up and spoiled it all.' He shook his head. 'With my record, I can hardly object to you having a life of your own, Ashley. And I won't stop you using this place either. But whoever you bring here, you're going to remember I had you here first.'

'You're disgusting!' His nearness was affecting her profoundly. Inwardly, she was trembling, starting to ache ...

'I'm sure you think so.' Jago picked her up in his arms and carried her back into the living room, depositing her full length on the big sheepskin rug in front of the empty fireplace. She struggled up on to an elbow.

'What are you doing?'

'Your memory can't be that poor,' he jibed, peeling the thin wool sweater he was wearing over his head and tossing it to one side. 'What I did last night, darling, with a few variations on the central theme, perhaps.' He dropped to one knee beside her, his hand moving with heart-stopping intimacy over her jean-clad thighs. She gasped and tried to twist away, but he was too quick for her, straddling her struggling body with one lithe movement.

'Some animation at last,' he commented. 'Last night I thought I was in bed with a marble statue.'

'Let go of me!' she spat at him. 'Get away from me, damn you!'

'Not a chance.' He had captured both her wrists in one hand, rendering her virtually powerless. Now he slid his hand under the midriff of the scarlet T-shirt, easing it upwards. His fingers found the fragile clip which fastened her bra in the delicate valley between her breasts, and twisted it open, so that the lace cups fell away, baring her. He bent, and she felt his mouth, warm and sensuous against her flesh, his tongue teasing one hardening nipple with deliberate eroticism. His lips paid tribute to her other breast, then drifted downward over her ribcage, and the flat plane of her stomach to the waistband of her jeans.

He lifted his head. His eyes, intent, slumbrous with desire, held hers making it impossible to look away.

He said huskily, 'You taste like heaven.'

He let go of her wrists so that he could free her completely from the tangle of her T-shirt, and she made no effort to fight him. Her skin was tingling, unbearably sensitised by the leisurely brush of his mouth.

Last night she had denied herself the pleasure he offered, her fear of the unknown bolstering her resistance. But she could no longer use her sexual ignorance as a barricade. Her senses were reminding her with compelling urgency just how Jago had felt inside her.

He kissed her mouth, parting her lips without haste, and with a little sob, she responded, shyly at first, then with increasing confidence as the kiss deepened, and demanded.

She twined her arms round his neck, holding him against her, enjoying the sensation of the hard wall of his chest against the softness of her breasts.

Jago took his lips from hers and began to plant tiny kisses on her face, tracing her hairline, her cheekbones, her closed eyes. She found she was revelling in the swift, sensuous caresses, her head turning restlessly. When his mouth covered hers again, she didn't shrink from its urgent mastery, but answered fire with breathless fire.

He lifted himself away from her and she felt his hand at the waistband of her jeans, and the downward rasp of her zip. She twined her arms round his neck as he eased her slenderness free of the clinging material, her body burning, melting as his fingers cupped her intimately before deftly disposing of the few inches of lace which still covered her.

She was quivering in every fibre of her being, eagerly awaiting his caress, but she was totally unprepared for the warmth of his mouth against her, exploring every sweet secret of her womanhood.

'No!' Ashley reared up in outrage and sheer panic.

'Hush,' he said. And, gently, 'It's all right.'

His hands stroked her trembling body, offering the physical reassurance of his touch, as if she was some small, frightened animal whom he was soothing to acceptance. As the shocked rigidity seeped out of her, he whispered, 'There's a journey into pleasure ahead of us, Ashley. This time I don't intend to travel alone.'

His lips touched her breasts, moving in insidious beguilement from the heated rosy peaks to the scented valley between, then laid a warm trail downwards over her abdomen. The lazy brush of his mouth tantalised and beckoned, drawing her from the shelter of her remaining inhibitions, so that when he regained his goal she was incapable of further resistance. Her head fell back on the softness of the rug, a little helpless sigh rising in her throat as she surrendered to the ripples of sensation spreading through her tingling body.

The ripples became waves, small fierce storms of delight driving her relentlessly towards some peak of pleasure as yet undreamed of.

There was a pulse beating within her, deep and savage as the universe. Nothing else existed, or ever had. The pulsation deepened unbearably, drew her down into some vortex, consumed her, then flung her out into a vast shimmering void.

Jago said, 'Now,' and took her.

Locked with him in the harsh, driving rhythm of his possession, new spasms convulsed her. She heard herself cry out, gasping for breath, torn apart by ecstasy—felt the great shudder of final consummation engulf him too.

Reality returned slowly. Ashley was aware of his weight on her, the unheated air of the flat striking a chill against her perspiring skin. Jago moved abruptly, lifting himself away from her, pushing his sweat-dampened hair back from his face.

Ashley lay still, watching him under her lashes. She wanted to tell him how much she loved him, but shyness paralysed her, making it impossible to speak. After all, he knew everything about her now. She had no secrets left, nor did she want to have. But the hangover of her old fears and reticences was still there, and she needed reassurance.

But the harsh, brooding expression on his face

offered her no comfort at all. Had she shocked him? she wondered. Had the wildness of her response confirmed that she was, in some way, abnormal?

She swallowed, trying to relax the taut muscles in her throat. She had to speak—to ask.

As if aware of her trembling regard, Jago turned his head slightly and looked at her, the hazel eyes expressionless as they brushed over her nakedness.

'So much for your Miss Frigidity act!' The firm mouth twisted as he reached for his clothes. 'So— who did you pretend I was? Witham, or one of the future dream lovers you plan to entertain here?'

The edge of contempt in his voice stung like a blow. With shaking hands, Ashley reached for her own scatter of garments, letting her dark hair swing forward to conceal her flushed, downbent face.

'A dream lover,' she said.

It was no more than the truth. Jago had always filled any dream of love she had ever possessed. It was her tragedy that he was the only man she had ever wanted, or ever would want, and she was going to have to live with that.

'My congratulations,' he said mockingly. 'I had no idea you had such a vivid imagination.'

He got to his feet and walked over to the window, staring out, his back turned to her, while Ashley huddled into her clothes. He said brusquely, 'Do you want me to drive you back to the Manor?'

'No, I'll use my own car.' She paused. 'I still have some things to see to here in town.'

She could hardly believe what was happening. Only a short while before, they had been united in a passionate intimacy she had never dreamed could exist. Now it was over, and they were back in the mundane world, as separate as they had ever been, talking banalities.

Jago shrugged. 'As you wish,' he said curtly. 'I'll see you at the house later.'

The door closed behind him, shutting her into the empty room, reminding her with bitter emphasis of all those other empty rooms which would face her one day—when their marriage was over.

She took her time over her errands, deliberately delaying the moment when she would have to return to the Manor, and all the problems which awaited her there. She tried to fill her mind with her plans for the morning room, poring over carpet samples and curtain fabrics, but she couldn't banish Jago from her brain, or the heated recollection of the passion they had shared from her memory. She had given him everything, and now she had to come to terms with the reality of how little her gift had been valued. After all, she told herself wretchedly, Jago was an expert lover, virile and exciting. To him, her capitulation would have been no more than his due. But it changed nothing between them.

Eventually she chose some ready-made curtains in an attractive shade of old rose, added cushion covers to match, and drove slowly back to the house through the lanes.

She took her purchases straight to the morning room. Emptied of its furniture, it already looked larger and lighter, she decided critically.

She fetched a chair from the dining room, and stood on it to take the old curtains down. It was a stretch, and the weight of the fabric made her arms ache, but she persevered. Her task achieved, it was comparatively easy to transfer the hooks to the new curtains, then she gathered up the folds of material and clambered back on her perch. But re-attaching the hooks to the waiting curtain rings was more difficult than she had anticipated. It was a fiddly task, and the chair began to feel more and more precarious as she struggled.

Ashley gritted her teeth, rising on tiptoe to secure the last hook. As she did so, the chair rocked alarmingly, and she gave a startled cry, lunging at the window frame to regain her balance.

From behind her Jago demanded glacially, 'What the hell do you think you're doing?'

His hands clamped round her waist, steadying her, and lifting her inexorably to the floor.

'Hanging curtains.' Mutinously, Ashley pulled herself free, her face flushing.

'I thought perhaps you were trying to hang yourself,' he said caustically. 'But I should warn you that fooling around on old chairs leads more often to a broken ankle than a broken neck. Why didn't you get Mrs Bolton to help you?'

'Because I don't like her.' Ashley bent and retrieved an errant hook from the carpet. 'As a matter of fact ...' She paused.

'Yes?'

She lifted her head defiantly. 'As a matter of fact,' she repeated, 'I've given her a month's notice.'

'Have you indeed?' Jago's brows snapped together in a frown. 'Don't you think that's something you should have discussed with me first?'

'You weren't there to ask,' she said coolly.

'Then you should have waited until I was,' he said grimly.

'I don't see why,' Ashley protested. 'There are other housekeepers in the world. She isn't indispensable.'

'Erica thinks she is,' he said quietly. 'So I'm afraid Mrs Bolton will have to be reinstated.'

'You can't be serious,' Ashley said, after a pause.

'Never more so.' His mouth twisted. 'I can't say Mrs Bolton is my flavour of the month either, but to fire her unceremoniously could cause all kinds of problems, which I'd prefer to avoid if possible.'

'You mean it would upset Erica?'

'You could say that.'

'And that, of course, must be avoided at all costs?' Ashley used sarcasm to mask the hurt.

'Yes.' The hazel eyes met hers directly. 'Ashley, there's something you have to understand ...'

'Oh, but I do understand—believe me, I do. In fact, the only thing that baffles me is why you married me, instead of waiting for her to finish her period of mourning, if that's what it is. In fact, there was very little need to wait at all.'

He shrugged, 'Oh, I think the conventions should be preserved—sometimes.'

'You surprise me.' Her voice sharpened. 'So— why did you marry me?' She stopped. 'Oh, but of course, there was Landons.'

'Exactly,' Jago said softly. 'Above and beyond all personal considerations, there was Landons.'

She twisted the hook in her fingers, bending it out of shape. 'So Mrs Bolton stays. Will you tell her, or am I expected to?'

'I'll speak to her myself.'

'Good.' Ashley bit her lip. 'And during the course of conversation, perhaps you could arrange for my things to be put back in the guest bedroom. After all, if Erica's feelings are so important to you, you can hardly upset her by sleeping with another woman.'

He shrugged again. 'I think she's more of a realist than you give her credit for,' he said. 'But your consideration for her amazes me, Ashley. I'm not sure she'd treat you quite so delicately, if she were in your place.'

'Perhaps.' She dragged a ghost of a smile from somewhere. 'I'll have to—wait and see, won't I? But in the meantime, I'd rather sleep alone.'

'I'm sure you would,' he said pleasantly. 'But I'm afraid I'm not prepared to gratify your whim. I've married you, Ashley, and I want you in my bed, physically at least, even if your heart and mind are elsewhere. But that doesn't mean you can repeat your ice-maiden act, however,' he added, with a touch of grimness. 'You proved very satisfactorily a few hours ago that you're subject to the same urges and lusts which drive ordinary mortals, so I won't settle for anything less in future.' He took her chin in his hand and looked down into her eyes. 'Try and freeze me away again, sweetheart, and you'll regret it.' His mouth twisted, and he gave the bare room around them a swift, comprehensive look. 'Meanwhile—enjoy your sanctuary.'

'I haven't one,' she said. She took a step forward. 'Jago, I know I made you angry when I broke off our engagement. Perhaps you expected me to be sophisticated enough to—take our relationship for what it was, and turn a blind eye to your other amusements. But haven't you had your revenge? How long do you expect me to go on—like this?'

He said levelly, 'Until I decide it's time to stop. I'll let you know when that is.'

Ashley moistened her lips with the tip of her tongue. 'When you're tired of me? Or when Erica comes back?'

'Now that would be telling,' he mocked her. 'But I'd say a little of both, wouldn't you?'

'Haven't you any mercy?' Her voice shook.

Jago shook his head slowly. 'I seem to be fresh

out of that particular commodity, especially when it involves spending my nights alone.' He laughed. 'But cheer up, my sweet. Look at your life with me like a balance sheet. Weigh the credit of keeping Landons inviolate against the debit of having to lend yourself to my unspeakable passions, once in a while. I'm sure you'll see where the profit lies.' He ran a caressing finger down the curve of her cheek. 'You always did, after all.'

'Thank you for reminding me,' she said quietly. 'That makes it all worth while, naturally.'

His eyes narrowed. 'I thought it might.' He bent and kissed her. It was only a breath of a caress, the merest brush of his mouth across hers, but it burned her like a brand.

He walked to the door and went out, without even a backward glance.

As, she supposed, he would, one day, walk away from her.

She sank down on to the shabby carpet, hugging her arms protectively across her breasts.

Oh, God, she thought achingly. What am I going to do?

CHAPTER NINE

'AND we look forward to meeting you on site to discuss your requirements in more detail. Yours, etc.' Ashley switched off her dictating machine and leaned back in her chair.

Another bread-and-butter reply successfully completed, she thought morosely. And very dull when used, as she was, to the real cut and thrust of decision-making.

She got up restlessly and went over to the window.

A week, she thought broodingly, since she had undertaken that reckless marriage. But they had proved seven of the most eventful days of her life. Although not, she was forced to concede, as far as her working life went. Jago was still keeping her, quite deliberately, on the fringe of things at the office. She was given routine tasks, but even these, she was aware, were scrutinised thoroughly.

For instance, she knew that this was the day when the final figure on the Craigmore tender would be decided, but that was the extent of her information. She had attended no meetings, nor received any memos on the subject, and in view of its importance to Landons' future, this was a ludicrous situation. Jago had imposed a tight new security régime on the whole building. There was a sense of urgency and purpose in the corridors these days that Ashley had to admit had not always been present over the past months, but that did not excuse the fact that she was excluded from the top-level decisions that were being taken about the company's future.

And when she had protested to Jago, insisting that she should be allowed to safeguard her interests, he had merely raised his eyebrows and drawled, 'Your interests are mine, darling. Don't you trust me to protect them?'

And had waited, mockingly, as the silence between them lengthened ...

There had been many such silences over the past week, Ashley thought unhappily. Silence when Mrs Bolton came to tell him that Mrs Marrick was on the phone and wished to speak to him—something which happened with monotonous regularity each evening, so that, almost unconsciously, Ashley was waiting for the shrill of the telephone bell.

Silence, when Jago vanished, sometimes for hours at a time, and returned volunteering no explanation.

And the most breathless silence of all when she awoke beside him in the morning to find him propped up on one elbow, watching her, the faint sardonic smile playing about his mouth reminding her more potently than any words could have done of the passion he had made her share the previous night.

She was allowed no respite. He made love to her with an erotic artistry which made her writhe in helpless shame when she recalled in daylight's sanity the depth of response he had drawn from her.

And she knew it must amuse him to contrast the cool self-contained image she maintained during working hours with the wild girl, sobbing with abandonment, whom he held in his arms each night. He took, she thought, an almost clinical pleasure in wringing every last ounce of sensation from her, leaving her drained and boneless on some barren shore of loneliness and need.

It was moments like these which made her want to turn to him, to beg words of love from him, even if they were only a pretence. It was moments like these which made her grateful for the silences which forbade any such disastrous impulse.

There had been other difficulties too, one of them Mrs Bolton's quiet but barely concealed triumph at the withdrawal of her notice. She had never actually said 'I told you so', but her attitude had implied it at every turn.

The only place where Ashley felt free of her encroaching presence was the morning room. Her furniture had arrived, and had been arranged to her satisfaction, so that part of the Manor felt like home at least. But it was a very small part. In the rest of the house, she still felt like an unwanted guest, and what it would be like when Erica returned she could only guess at and dread.

She had asked Jago tentatively whether she could have a dog, only to have the suggestion vetoed. Jago had been quite blunt about it. Erica, it seemed, couldn't stand dogs and hadn't allowed Giles to have his elderly retriever in the house, in case Polly did some unnamed damage to the expensive furnishings.

'I see.' Ashley had lifted her chin.

'I don't think you do,' Jago had returned wearily. 'But, for the time being, I'd be grateful if you'd respect her wishes. Believe me, it would make things very much easier.'

'I believe you.' Ashley turned away, icily masking her hurt and disappointment. 'God forbid that I should do anything to upset your cosy little applecart!'

'Amen to that.' Jago's voice followed her crisply. 'Just for once, Ashley, will you credit me with knowing what I'm doing?'

A bitter smile touched the corners of her mouth. 'I've always credited you with that, Jago. I'm sure you plan every move you make. I just wish I could have avoided being involved in your machinations.'

'And so do I.' His voice bit. 'But at the moment, it's a situation we're stuck with, so kindly make the best of it, as I'm doing.'

It had been a sharp little confrontation, and it had shaken Ashley to realise that, in spite of his unconcealed enjoyment of her body, Jago was also ill at ease in their taut relationship. It had depressed her too, and she shivered a little now as she stared unseeingly down at the sunlit street below.

A brief tap at her door made her start, and she turned quickly, forcing a smile as Henry Brett came in.

'Sorry to interrupt if you're busy,' he said. 'But Shelagh wanted me to remind you that you're coming to dinner tonight.'

'I hadn't forgotten.' Ashley walked back to her desk and sat down. 'We're both looking forward to it.'

Which was not strictly true, she thought ruefully. When she had mentioned the invitation to Jago he had lapsed into frowning silence for a while, then asked abruptly if they could make some excuse.

'No.' She had shaken her head vehemently. 'Henry and Shelagh are old friends of mine. He's looked after me like an uncle ever since my father died, and they'd be hurt if we turned them down. I'll go on my own, if you prefer,' she had added defiantly.

His frown had deepened. 'There's no need for

that,' he said. 'If you've already accepted for both of us, then of course we'll go.'

And the matter had been left there.

'You look pale,' Henry said, frowning a little. 'I hope you're not overworking.'

'Far from it.' Ashley waved a hand at the paperwork in front of her with a semblance of gaiety. 'As a matter of fact, I've already filled today's quota. It doesn't take a great deal of effort, I promise you. In fact a properly programmed robot could do it.'

Henry's face grew thunderous. 'It's a disgrace!' he muttered. 'Ashley, my dear, I'm so sorry, but ...'

'But you did warn me,' she completed for him with a faint grimace. 'Only I can't say I expected to be relegated to the Second Division quite so fast!'

'If it's any consolation, you're not the only one,' Henry said sourly. 'Your husband has instructed me to re-examine the financial and working structure of the entire company, and report on how they could be updated and improved. And he wants it yesterday.'

Ashley looked at him with compunction. Henry looked tired, she thought, and harassed. If she could get Shelagh on her own tonight, she would suggest they went away for a holiday. He looked as if he was in desperate need of a complete break. Immersed in her own troubles, she had forgotten what a fraught time this had been for him too. He'd had to bear the brunt of the early pressure from Marshalls, and she must not forget it.

She asked tentatively, 'Do you need extra help? We could get you a temp, or more than one. It's what we've always done in the past.'

Henry shook his head. '"Past" is the operative

word, my dear. Jago has already made it clear that
he regards this particular project as being fully
within the present capabilities of my department—
and I quote.' He gave an irritable sigh, pushing a
hand through his thinning hair. 'I suppose he feels
if I'm drowning in a sea of paperwork and statistics,
I won't have a chance to throw a spanner in any of
his works.'

'Why should he think you want to do that?' asked
Ashley, frowning a little in her turn.

He shrugged. 'God knows—except that I'm one
of the leftovers from your father's era and therefore
can't be expected to approve of the changes
he's making to Landons. Silas believed in open
management. Your husband, in contrast, holds his
cards so close to his chest, it's difficult to know
whether he's even worked out their value himself.'
He snorted. 'All this secrecy! What's he afraid of?'

She said slowly, 'Jago thinks we've been losing
too many contracts lately.'

'And what, precisely, does he blame for that?'
Henry demanded sharply.

'I don't know.' Ashley began to play with the cap
of her pen. 'But perhaps he's right, Henry. Perhaps
our security has been lax—I don't know.' She
sighed. 'And maybe he blames me for it, perhaps
that's why ...' She stopped.

'What were you going to say?'

She spread her hands helplessly. 'Perhaps that's
why he makes sure I don't get access to anything
important these days.'

'Haven't you asked him?'

Ashley shifted some of the papers on her desk,
her movements restless and jerky. 'Not in so many
words,' she said, after a pause. 'It isn't as easy as
that.'

'I can believe that,' said Henry with a snap. 'Surely he doesn't suspect you of—industrial espionage?'

She smiled drearily. 'I doubt it. I think he regards me as simply inefficient, which in some ways is worse.'

'My dear girl!' he sounded shocked. 'Nothing could be further from the truth. You mustn't allow Jago to treat you like a cipher. You need to—stand up for your rights. You were Silas' daughter before you were his wife, after all.'

'Provoking mutiny, Henry?' She smiled with an effort. 'You surprise me.'

'I don't see why.' He shook his head. 'I was against this ill-advised marriage from the first, as you know. I feel you allowed yourself to be rushed into it without giving the consequences sufficient thought.' He paused. 'I can see you're not happy—indeed how could you be?—and it worries me.'

'Don't be worried.' She gave him an affectionate but searching glance. 'All marriages have their—teething troubles, I suppose, but you mustn't be concerned. As it is, you look as if you haven't been sleeping properly for weeks. I hope that isn't on my account.'

'No—no.' Henry shook his head vaguely as if his thoughts were elsewhere. 'It's just all this extra work. I think I must be getting old.' His lips pursed. 'And Jago requires a daily report on my progress.'

She said quietly, 'It doesn't sound as if relations are very good anywhere along the line. Perhaps this dinner party will—restore things a little. After all, we're working for a common cause.'

'Are we?' he asked heavily. 'Sometimes I get the impression—forgive me, Ashley—that your husband is working for himself alone. But perhaps tonight will promote a better atmosphere. I certainly hope so.'

As he reached the door, Ashley said casually, 'Henry, have you seen the final tender figure for the Craigmore project?'

He turned abruptly. 'No—no, I haven't. Why do you ask?'

There was an edge to his voice that bewildered her. 'Because I haven't seen it either, that's all. And both of us would normally have done so.'

He gave a short laugh. 'Tenders are tantamount to classified documents these days. Haven't you been reading your memos? I don't think either of us are on Jago's "need to know" list.'

'But that's quite ridiculous!' Ashley stood up with resolution. 'I'm going to speak to him about it now. After all, both of us were in on that project from the first.'

'So we were,' he said. 'But times have changed. It's been made clear to me that I'm no longer involved in that side of things. But don't let me stop you trying,' he added drily. 'Do you know the combination of that safe of Jago's?'

She flushed. 'No—but he has to let me see the tender. He must.'

'I hope he will,' said Henry. 'But I wouldn't count on it, my dear. And there's no point in tackling him about it at once, because he's not there. When I rang his office just now, his girl said he'd already left for an early lunch appointment. And he's pretty tied up this afternoon, it seems. I'm to leave my report on his desk.' He patted the folder under his arm.

'I'll take it,' said Ashley, putting out her hand. 'And I'll tell Sue to fit me in between the other appointments, if that's what it takes.'

But when she reached Jago's office, it was to find

it deserted. Ashley stood looking round her in slight
perplexity. It was unusual not to find Sue at her
post. In the short time she had been working for
Jago, she had established herself as an excellent
dragon, and the office was rarely unoccupied.

Ashley wrote a brief note, requesting a few
minutes of Jago's time when he got back from
lunch, and propped it in Sue's typewriter. Then she
glanced across at Jago's desk. It was strewn with
papers, which, again, was unusual, as he preferred
to work without clutter. And lying on top of the
papers was one of the distinctive blue and gold
folders in which Landons sent out their tenders.

Ashley's brows drew together. She went over and
picked it up, skimming through the contents. Sure
enough, it was the Craigmore tender, she realised
in total bewilderment. But in view of Jago's
strictness about security, what on earth was it doing
here where anyone could see it?

Determinedly she picked it up, dropping Henry's
report in its place, and turned towards the door.
That would be something else she would take up
with Jago when he came back from lunch.

As she went back towards her own room, she
spotted Henry talking to the Chief Accountant. She
gave him a small wave, drew his attention to the
folder she was carrying, and gave him a small,
triumphant thumbs up signal.

She sat down at her desk and began to go through
the figures. They were competently and concisely
put together, she thought, but the actual result
wasn't so different from her own tentative figure.

No wonder he didn't want to show it to me, she
thought rather bitterly. I might have said 'I told
you so'.

She sighed, closing the folder, and buried her

face in her hands for a moment. Wasn't it bad
enough that she and Jago were at odds in their
private life? Did the fight have to carry over into
the business world as well? Somehow she would
have to convince him that she still had a contribution
to make at Landons.

The buzz of her telephone made her jump. Katie
said, 'There's a Mr Hollings on the line for you,
Mrs Marrick. Shall I put him through?'

Ashley's brows lifted incredulously. After a pause,
she queried, 'Are you sure the switchboard got the
name right, Katie?'

'Yes.' Katie hesitated. 'Is it someone you'd rather
not speak to?'

A thousand times, yes, Ashley thought wryly.
Aloud, she said, 'It's all right, I'll speak to him.'

'You're guarded well,' was Paul Hollings' greeting.
He sounded frankly amused.

'I think sometimes I need to be,' she said shortly.
'What can I do for you, Mr Hollings?'

'Always so formal,' he said mournfully. 'Can't
you bring yourself to call me Paul?'

'I doubt it,' she said. 'And I'm rather too busy
for social chit-chat, so if you don't mind ...'

'Of course,' he said. 'This is a big day for both of
us. The deadline for the Craigmore tender, no less.
I hope you're prepared to accept defeat gracefully,
Ashley.'

'I'm not prepared to accept it at all,' she snapped.

He laughed. 'I can believe that! Let's call a truce,
and have lunch together.'

'Why should I do any such thing?'

'Because I happen to be in the neighbourhood,
and because you, presumably, need to eat.' He
paused. 'Unless you're otherwise engaged, of course.
Won't Jago let you off the leash for once, darling?'

'Jago's not here,' she said, and could have bitten her tongue out.

'Better and better,' he said softly. 'That's how I like inconvenient husbands—absent. So will you take pity on me, and grace my lonely lunch table?'

Ashley nibbled at her thumbnail, torn between a desire to slam the phone down and the need to know what he was up to. Curiosity won.

'Where shall I meet you?' she asked.

'There's rather a good roadhouse out towards Ashbrook, I'm told.'

'There is indeed,' Ashley said lightly. 'We built it.'

'Then I'm sure it can be trusted not to come crashing round our ears while we eat,' he said. 'Shall we say—half an hour?'

She agreed, and heard the click as his line disconnected.

She replaced her own receiver slowly. Paul Hollings had sent flowers with a polite note to thank her for her hospitality, but there had been nothing to suggest that he intended any further social contact between them. Yet—now this.

She went into the washroom and renewed her lipstick, looking at herself critically. She was wearing one of her discreet, anonymous office suits today, in navy. He would find her a very different proposition from the exotic creature in emerald green he'd met the previous week, she thought, her mouth curling in faint amusement as she combed her hair.

The car park at the roadhouse was filling up when she arrived, but she managed to wangle her car into a space near the front door. An enquiry at the reception desk in the foyer told her that Mr Hollings was waiting for her in the cocktail bar.

He got to his feet, and came to meet her smiling. 'I daren't tell you that you look as lovely as ever,' he said, as he ordered her the glass of white wine she requested. 'I'm sure you have some dagger-like reply all prepared.'

His quizzical look forced a laugh from her. 'You're learning!'

'I try.' Paul lifted his glass to her. 'Here's to a closer relationship—in every way.'

She lifted an eyebrow. 'I think I'll drink to your health,' she said. 'It sounds safer.'

'Always so cautious,' he sighed. 'How can I make you trust me? Get you to see that being taken over by my company isn't the worst thing that could happen?'

Ashley took a composed sip of her wine. 'You can't,' she said succinctly.

'You're really determined, aren't you?' he said softly. 'But so am I. Don't you think we should be looking for some kind of compromise?'

'I don't think so.' Ashley kept her voice level. 'You see, Mr Hollings, your company fails to meet any of the standards my father fought all his life to maintain. I refuse to stand back and allow you to take over his company, and use its reputation for your own ends.'

'You don't pull your punches,' he said wryly. 'But I like that. I admire a lady who doesn't know when she's beaten.'

'Is that what I am?'

'I'm afraid so. The Craigmore tender is as good as ours, and without it Landons will be in trouble. You can't deny that.' She remained silent, and he went on, 'Now I'm prepared to renew our earlier offer for Landons' shares on the understanding you call an emergency board meeting and recommend urgent acceptance of our offer.' He shrugged. 'I'd say that was an offer you couldn't refuse.'

'I wouldn't be too sure.' She set her glass back on the table. 'You're beginning to annoy me, Mr Hollings. I think I'll forgo lunch and go back to my crumbling business.'

'I'm sorry.' His tone altered, and he put a hand on her arm. 'If I swear not to raise the subject again, will you stay?'

Ashley sighed. 'I don't know why you should want me to,' she pointed out.

'Because when your marriage to Jago breaks up, I want to be around to pick up the pieces,' Paul Hollings said calmly, and signalled to the waiter to take their order.

Dazedly, Ashley opted for pâté, followed by poached salmon with a side salad, and heard her companion order the same.

When the waiter had moved away, she said, 'I think you must be out of your mind!'

He shook his head. 'On the contrary. You're a beautiful girl, Ashley Landon, and you're not happy. But then how could you be? On your own admission, your marriage was a put up job to pacify your board of directors. You deserve better than that.'

'From you?' she raised a caustic eyebrow.

'Why not? I've made my matrimonial mistake and paid for it. I won't be trapped into the same error again. I didn't enjoy divorce, but it taught me quite a lot.' He gave her a straight look. 'You have to learn to turn your back on failure, Ashley, whether in business or in your private life.'

'I don't regard my marriage as a failure,' she said steadily. 'It was—a means to an end, that's all, and it's worked.'

'Loyal but misguided,' Paul Hollings said mockingly, and began to study the wine list.

Ashley had never felt less hungry in her life, but it was almost a relief when the head waiter arrived to conduct them to their table in the green and gilt dining room.

As she'd noticed on her few earlier visits, the male presence predominated in the dining room, and she was aware of frankly curious stares as she was escorted to her table.

Aware, with a prickle of sensitivity, of something more than curiosity in the atmosphere. As the waiter shook out her napkin and began to pour the wine, she glanced casually round—and froze.

From a table intimately secluded in a corner, Jago looked back at her, his eyes cold with angry conjecture. She saw his companion, and the way she was leaning towards him, her face wreathed in smiles, saw the champagne bottle nestling in ice beside their table.

Ashley felt her nails curling into claws beneath the shelter of the tablecloth. Her reaction was savage, primitive, shocking. Pain was striking at her, and she wanted to inflict pain in turn—smash that celebratory bottle over Erica's smooth blonde head, scratch the triumph from her face.

Mark them both, she thought in agony, as they've marked me!

With a jolt, she pulled herself together. Paul Hollings, luckily, was sitting with his back turned to that corner, and hadn't, she would swear, noticed its occupants. Or at least she prayed he hadn't. She would have to make sure that his attention stayed riveted—on her.

'It all looks delicious,' she said lightly. 'Perhaps we should forget our irreconcilable differences for the next hour, and simply enjoy ourselves?' She made it sound like an invitation, inwardly despising herself.

He smiled back, letting his eyes linger with undisguised appreciation on her lips and breasts. Oh God, he thought he was so damned irresistible!

He said softly, 'I ask for nothing more—at the moment.' He raised his glass. 'I say again—here's to our closer relationship.'

She lowered her lashes demurely. 'In every way,' she agreed, deliberately echoing his own words, noting the gleam in his eyes as he registered the fact.

She tasted her pâté, making appreciative noises, watching him relax and bask in her approval. A basking shark, she thought detachedly. Because she didn't believe one of the reasons he'd formulated for inviting her to lunch. She didn't doubt he still wanted to acquire Landons, and would be prepared to go to any lengths to do so, but his renewed offer made no sense. Why pay a high price for a company he intended to drive into the ground? As for his other proposition, she supposed that as a young wife trapped in a marriage of convenience she was intended to be grateful for his sexual interest in her, and flattered by it.

She would have, she thought, to find some way of convincing him once and for all that she wasn't interested in any offer he might make, either personal or professional.

The salmon arrived, and hollandaise sauce was offered.

Paul Hollings was talking, making conversation, and doing it well, canvassing her views on music, the theatre and current affairs. Trying to establish common ground, Ashley thought idly, and if she'd been as naïve as he thought, or even halfway interested in him, this lunch could have been one big thrill from start to finish.

As it was, each mouthful was a profound effort, even though the food was good, and the wine like silk against the taut dryness of her throat.

Looking past him, she saw that Jago was preparing to leave, signing the bill, and helping Erica into her jacket. She watched them walk towards the door, Jago's head bent attentively towards his companion, who was chatting vivaciously, clearly revelling in the glances she was attracting. He did not even spare Ashley a glance. As they disappeared through the arched doorway, Ashley sank back in her chair, aware she was trembling violently.

'Is something the matter?' Paul Hollings had stopped in mid-eulogy of the Royal Shakespeare Company and was studying her with bewilderment.

'Everything's wonderful,' she said. 'It was a lovely meal. You must forgive me if I tear myself away.'

If he hadn't practised so hard at being suave, his jaw would have dropped. He made a good recovery. 'Surely you don't have to go yet? There's dessert— and coffee. Besides—' he gave her a smile designed to melt her bones, 'I had—plans for this afternoon.'

'I'm sorry.' Ashley got to her feet, shaking her head. 'I'm going to be busy this afternoon. And so are you. You have a visit to the dry cleaners to fit in, for one thing.'

This time he looked really blank. 'I don't follow you ...'

'Good,' said Ashley. 'Let's keep it that way.' She reached for the sauce boat and poured the remains of the hollandaise sauce all over him.

And in the most profound silence since the beginning of the world, she walked out of the restaurant.

CHAPTER TEN

SHE was still shaking inside when she got back to the office. She buzzed Jago immediately, but it was Sue who replied, informing her that he hadn't returned from lunch yet.

Ashley said with an assumption of calm, 'Please let me know as soon as he returns.'

Each time her buzzer sounded, she tensed, but it was never the message she was waiting for. Incredulously, she realised that almost two hours had passed. She could only suppose that as she'd caught Jago with Erica publicly, he saw no reason to maintain any kind of subterfuge.

She paced up and down, dry-eyed, trying to close her mind against insidious images of Jago in bed with Erica, their bodies moulded together in passion. Unbearable, hateful images scalding against her closed eyelids.

She said aloud, 'I can't go on like this.' And at that moment, the buzzer sounded, and Sue's voice said, 'Mrs Marrick? Is it convenient for you to come along, please?'

She was vanishing discreetly as Ashley arrived. Jago's face was like a mask, but he could not disguise the angry glitter in his eyes as he rose to greet her.

He said icily, 'I hope you had a pleasant lunch.'

'It had its moments.' She was determined to play it cool. She wanted to scream accusations, burst into tears, stamp and throw things, but this was not the time or the place.

'I'm sure it did.' His mouth was tight-lipped. His voice would have cut chips from granite. 'You don't care to explain what you were doing there with him?'

Ashley shrugged. 'I'm astonished you should want to know. Especially when I could ask you the same thing—about her.'

'Ask,' he grated. 'I'm perfectly willing to tell you.'

'You clearly regard frankness about your affairs as some sort of virtue,' Ashley said quietly. 'It's a view I don't happen to share. I don't want to know, Jago. You're a free agent, you can have lunch with whomever you please. But I have the same right too.' She put the Craigmore file down on the desk in front of him. 'I didn't come here to cross-examine you. I came to return this.'

His brows snapped together. 'Where the hell did you get this?' he almost snarled.

'It was lying about on your desk,' she said. 'Obviously you were in too much of a hurry to get to your lunch engagement to bother with your usual security precautions.'

Oh hell! she thought furiously. That last remark had all the elements of a jealous whine.

But Jago seemed oblivious to its implications. He cursed savagely and slapped the folder with a clenched fist. Then he looked up at her. 'And may I know where it's been since you—acquired it?'

'I put it in my desk drawer. I think it was as safe there as it was here.'

'Hmm.' His expression was abstracted. 'Did anyone know you had it? Did you discuss it with anyone?'

'With Paul Hollings, for instance?' she asked.

'You know better than that.'

His glance was loaded. 'I'm not sure I know anything any more. But O.K., I acquit you of Hollings. However I really need to know whether you discussed the contents of this file with anyone in this building.'

'No,' she said shortly. 'Is that what you wanted to hear?'

Jago sighed. 'Not particularly,' he returned curtly. 'It's just an extra complication which I didn't need.'

'I haven't the vaguest idea what you're talking about.'

'I don't suppose you have.' His mouth curled. 'And that's just how I wanted it. You on the outside, uninvolved.'

'And what about my own wishes?' Ashley demanded. 'I'm sick of being treated like an office junior!'

'Is that how you see yourself?' he asked flatly. 'I don't think office juniors get wined and dined by our main business rivals, but I could be wrong.' He paused. 'Did he mention the Craigmore project to you while you were playing footsie over the prawn cocktails?'

'We had other more important things to discuss.'

'Like the fact that he fancies you?' Jago asked contemptuously. 'Don't let it go to your head, darling. Because you'd be one of a long line, Ashley, and he's a bigger bastard than I am.'

'I find that hard to believe,' she said. 'But as it happens I wouldn't have the gallant Mr Hollings on toast.' In spite of her wretchedness, a golden memory warmed her, and a reluctant smile curved her mouth. 'Or served up with hollandaise sauce.' She glanced at her watch. 'How time does fly! Unless you have any other letters you'd like me to answer, I think I'll go back to the house. Please don't forget we're having dinner with the Bretts this evening.'

Jago came round the big desk and caught at her arm, halting her. 'You're not leaving yet. There are things we need to have a serious talk about.'

She felt the warm pressure of his fingers through her clothes as though she'd been naked, and pulled herself free, her face furious, her eyes gleaming cat-like. 'Take your hands off me!'

'That has a familiar ring,' he said insolently. 'Only it doesn't work any more, remember?' He took her hand, his thumb smoothing the gold of her wedding ring. He said quietly, 'You can't get away from me so easily this time, Ashley. You can't send this back by messenger, and call it a day.'

'I'm aware of that.' Her senses were jumping, her nerve-endings going mad as they always did even at his lightest touch. 'But I'll do whatever I need to do to be free again.' With a flood of relief, she heard Sue's voice in the corridor outside, and snatched her hand away.

As the door opened, she turned and smiled at the secretary. 'I'm just leaving,' she said brightly. 'Don't let him work late tonight, Sue. We have a dinner engagement.'

There was an angry flush staining Jago's cheek-bones as he turned away. He said, 'Then I'd better not waste any more time. Get your notebook, Sue.'

Ashley managed to keep her step jaunty as she left the room, but she slowed when she reached the corridor, almost stumbling into the wall, as she fought for control. Tears she dared not shed were stinging her eyes, and every breath she drew seemed torn from her lungs. The few yards to her own office seemed endless, a punishing marathon performance.

As she went in, Katie was just putting down the telephone. Her eyes widened as she looked at Ashley. 'Are you all right, Mrs Marrick? You look terribly pale.'

'I have a slight headache,' Ashley managed. 'I don't think I'll drive myself home tonight, Katie. Perhaps you'd get me a taxi.'

'Right away,' the girl said, buzzing Reception, but her expression was still puzzled.

Ashley's head was aching in real earnest by the time the taxi deposited her at the Manor. She paid off the driver and walked quickly inside and straight up to her room. She wanted some tea, but if she rang for any, or even went to the kitchen, she would be bound to encounter Mrs Bolton, and she wasn't up to dealing with any of the older woman's little pinpricks tonight.

She took some paracetamol and lay down on the bed, deliberately relaxing every muscle. She would get through the evening ahead, somehow, and then she would go away for the weekend somewhere where she could think, make herself face what she had to do next. She supposed she would have to see a solicitor, although inwardly she cringed from the idea of having to tell old Mr Whincliffe who had always looked after Silas' affairs that her marriage was over almost before it had begun.

She'd heard there were law firms which specialised in divorce. She would try and find out more, consult such a firm, perhaps. They would know how to make things easy for her. She made a little harsh noise in her throat. Easy? she asked herself bitterly. What was simple about cutting the heart out of her body?

She sighed helplessly, closing her eyes as a great

wave of weariness swept over her, and almost before she knew it, she had fallen asleep.

When she awoke, it was getting dark, and she sat up abruptly, peering at her watch, an exclamation escaping her lips as she saw what the time was.

She swung herself off the bed and went to the wardrobe, giving the rail of dresses a hurried scan. The last thing she wanted was to go to a dinner party, but after tomorrow at least she would be able to stop pretending, she thought, pulling one of the dresses off its hanger. Although not new, it was a favourite of hers, black lace, low-necked and long-sleeved over a sleek taffeta underskirt, with a sophistication she needed tonight to boost her confidence.

She looked at her watch again. Where was Jago? she wondered. If he didn't hurry, they were going to be late, or was that what he intended? Or did he mean to come back at all? The possibility that he might have decided to end their marriage there and then hit her with the force of a blow. She laid the dress across the bed and went into the bathroom, turning on the shower. She wouldn't think about that. She would behave as if this was a conventional evening in a normal marriage, and get ready for her party.

The warm rush of the water felt like soothing balm on her skin. With a little sigh she reached for the soap, then cried out as the cubicle door opened abruptly.

Jago said pleasantly, 'Sorry I'm late, darling. Had you given me up? Let's save time and water and shower together.'

He took the soap from her slackened grasp, and began to lather her shoulders and breasts, shocking her back to life and speech.

'Get out of here!'

'Nonsense,' Jago said mockingly. 'Do you realise we've been married just over a week, and you've not washed my back for me yet?'

'Nor will I.' Ashley set her teeth, pushing away his caressing tantalising hand which was straying down over her stomach. 'If you won't get out of here, then I will!'

'Your wish is my command.' Jago reached up and switched off the spray, then lifted her out of the cubicle, scooping up the towel she'd left waiting as he did so, and muffling her in its folds. She was pinioned against him, her arms shrouded in the clinging towel, or she would have hit him. Her feet kicked wildly at his wet shins as he carried her.

'Put me down, damn you!'

'When I'm good and ready.' He dropped her on to the bed, kneeling over her while he pulled the wet towel away. Ashley read the purpose in his face, and began to struggle more violently.

'Let me go!'

Jago shook his head slowly. 'That isn't what either of us wants.' He framed her furious face in his hands, and bent and kissed her mouth, not gently, almost forcing her lips apart.

When she could speak again, she said huskily, 'You disgust me. Wasn't this afternoon's episode enough for you? How many women do you need at a time?'

'For now, I want you,' he said. 'And I thought you didn't want to discuss this afternoon.'

He kissed her again, his hands ridding her of the towel completely, his fingers trailing the length of her naked body, stroking and inciting. She was aware of his mastery, alive and responsive to the dark magic he was weaving round her, and against which she had no defence. With a sob she put her face against his shoulder, tasting the cool dampness of his skin.

He said her name, and entered her, their fusion explosive, with a hint of savagery. Her taking was as deep and urgent as his own, her need as compelling. There was no mercy in him, and she wanted none.

Nothing existed in the world but this man, hers in the act of love if in no other way. The damp, silken brush of his skin against hers, each heated male thrust into her satin warmth were driving her beyond reason, beyond coherent thought to some deep and dreamless void. She was his mate, his counterpart, offering total completion, as her body arched and twisted beneath his, her shallow, frantic breathing echoing the harsh rasp of his own. Her flesh was wrenched, torn apart by sensation. Clinging to each other, mouths and bodies locked together, they fell headlong through time and space into the void.

Normality returned slowly. Ashley was floating somewhere, her whole body languid and luxuriant, after the ferocity of culmination. She felt Jago leave her, lift himself away from her, and her eyes flew open, enormous, brilliant in her flushed face as she looked up at him.

His voice was cool, ironic. 'I'm afraid we're going to be late for Henry's dinner party.'

He swung himself off the bed and went into the bathroom, and presently she heard water running. Ashley stayed where she was. She doubted if she was capable of movement. She'd wanted him to stay in her arms. Perhaps then they could have talked, reached some kind of understanding.

As he came back into the bedroom and walked

over to the long line of panelled wardrobes, she lifted herself on to one elbow.

She said softly, 'Must we go?'

He didn't even look at her. He said crisply, 'Unfortunately, it can't be avoided.'

He was dressing, pulling on his clothes with swift economical movements.

She felt humiliated, raging at herself because she had offered and been rejected. She collected her own things together and dressed in the bathroom, the door between them closed, as if the dark, sensual madness of the last few minutes had never happened. She made sure that her make-up was immaculate, but there was nothing she could do to hide the heady glow in her eyes, or tone down her love-warmed skin.

Jago was waiting, with obvious impatience, when she finally emerged. It was the first time she had worn this dress since their marriage, and she waited for him to say something, give some sign of approval.

He said brusquely, 'Shall we be going? I've brought the car round.'

There was a tension about him, she thought as they drove in silence to the Bretts'. There was a grimness about the set of his mouth which she could not explain—unless he was regretting have made love to her. Perhaps he was feeling guilty at having betrayed Erica, she thought painfully.

Almost before the car had stopped, the door was open and Shelagh was waiting to welcome them, her face wreathed in smiles.

'Of course you're not late,' she dismissed. 'And you both look marvellous. I think marriage agrees with you, Ashley.'

Ashley made herself smile in response, aware of

Jago's swift, sardonic glance.

'Where's Colin this evening?' she asked, glancing round the pleasant living room.

'He's gone to spend the weekend with a friend.' Shelagh cast her eyes to heaven. 'They're supposed to be studying together, but if I know them they'll be listening to heavy metal records, rather than getting to grips with Chaucer.'

'Oh, Colin will pass,' Ashley said with a shrug. 'He has Jeanne's example to follow, after all. He can't let a girl best him.'

'His thinking does run along those lines,' Shelagh agreed, grinning. 'One way he could improve on her performance is by writing a few more letters home when he gets to university. Jeanne sometimes lets weeks go by without a word, and then we get a few scrawled lines.'

'She's snowed under with work,' Henry broke in, as he poured sherry. 'You mustn't fuss so. She's all right.'

'It's natural to worry,' Jago said quietly. 'Do you never go to visit her, Mrs Brett?'

'Oh, please call me Shelagh.' She took the glass her husband handed to her. 'I went to see her in her first year, to make sure she was all right. But each time I've planned to go this year, something seems to have happened to prevent it. But Henry's been a couple of times, haven't you, darling?' Her face clouded. 'It was an awful blow when she didn't come home for Christmas, but she'd got this vacation job in a hotel, and they couldn't spare her.'

'I think we'll change the subject,' Henry said brusquely. 'There's nothing more boring for guests than hearing long stories about other people's offspring.'

Ashley saw Jago give him a long considering look. Talk turned to the economic situation, and after a while Shelagh excused herself to go to the kitchen. Ashley followed.

'I hope this evening isn't going to be a strain for you,' she said with a slight sigh. 'Jago isn't exactly Henry's favourite person at the moment.'

Shelagh tasted the soup simmering on the stove and added a pinch of salt. She gave Ashley a wry look. 'I don't think anyone's Henry's favourite at the moment! I don't know what's the matter with him these days. According to Betty next door it's the male menopause.' She frowned. 'But I thought that meant having affairs with girls half his age.'

Ashley laughed. 'I don't think you need to worry about that,' she said affectionately. 'I'm sure Henry's never looked at another woman.'

'No, he's always been a family man,' Shelagh agreed. 'But part of being that was his temperament. He always used to be so cheerful and even-tempered, even during the children's squabbles and adolescence. Now, he seems like a stranger much of the time.'

'Perhaps he's still worried about how things are going at work,' Ashley suggested. 'We're not out of the wood yet, by any means.'

'But he always used to talk about the office,' Shelagh pointed out. 'Now it seems to be a taboo subject—and not the only one.' She squared her shoulders determinedly. 'Let's think about food instead. If you've come out here to help, you could keep an eye on those croutons for me.'

The meal was excellent. Shelagh, Ashley thought, was a heavenly cook of the stockpot, substantial helping variety, and tonight she had excelled herself with a dish of small spring chickens braised in wine, and other delights. Ashley usually amused herself by trying to distinguish the various herbs and flavourings that went into each dish, but then previous dinner parties at Shelagh and Henry's had always been relaxed affairs. But tonight's gathering could in no way be described as that, she realised unhappily. There was tension in the air, almost tangibly. Jago and Henry were being civil to each other, she thought vexedly, but little more. They were more like antagonists weighing each other up before some duel than working colleagues or a host with an important guest. Shelagh was clearly making a determined effort to make the evening go well and Ashley made herself rally round in support. But their efforts only seemed to underline the basic lack of rapport between their husbands.

'Some brandy with your coffee?' asked Henry when they returned to the big sitting room, and the log fire crackling on the hearth.

'Thank you,' Jago nodded. He turned to Shelagh. 'That was the most delicious meal,' he told her. 'I shall never doubt my wife's eulogies again. I would hate to have missed it, although at one time it seemed possible—it's been one of those days, I'm afraid.' He paused. 'Has Henry told you anything about the Craigmore project?'

Shelagh's brow wrinkled. 'Not that I recall.'

'It's a contract we're tendering for,' Jago told her. 'A big one, and vital to our future. It had to go off today. And I'm afraid it kept me late at the office.'

Ashley put down her coffee cup. 'But it was ready this morning,' she protested.

'Not quite,' Jago said quietly. 'You see, I wasn't altogether happy with the final figure we'd arrived at, so I changed it, quite drastically, before it went off.'

There was a crash, as the brandy decanter slipped from Henry's hand and landed on the parquet floor, its contents spilling towards the thick Chinese carpet.

Ashley's mouth was suddenly dry, her heart thumping. She was looking at Henry. They were all looking at Henry, and seeing, as she did, the fear, the wretchedness, and the overwhelming guilt in his pale face.

Shelagh began uncertainly, 'Darling ...' but Jago cut in smoothly.

'Ash, take Shelagh to the kitchen and find something to clear up this mess. Henry and I have to talk.'

CHAPTER ELEVEN

'It was heroin,' Henry said. It was a long time later, and they were all together in the sitting room. He was on the sofa, Shelagh beside him, pale but dry-eyed, twisting a handkerchief in restless fingers. 'I was as worried as Shelagh when Jeanne stopped writing, so I went up to see her without telling anyone.

'To be honest, I thought she might have got herself pregnant. I'd met this fellow she was involved with on a previous visit, and I didn't like him or any of his friends. I could see at once that she was different, but at first I didn't know why.' He paused. 'I should have known, of course. They spell it out for you these days—the signs, the danger signals, but somehow you always think in terms of other people's children—never your own ...' He broke off, his voice cracking slightly.

Then he resumed, more quietly, 'When I realised what was happening, I went a bit mad, I think. She'd run up this massive overdraft at the bank to pay for drugs, and they were pressuring her about it. She'd been stealing from shops too—it was only a miracle she hadn't been caught—prosecuted ...' He swallowed. 'She wanted to stop—she promised she did, and I wanted her to have a chance. After all, she was brilliant. Everyone said so. I couldn't let all that go to waste.' He lifted his head, almost defiantly, 'I couldn't!'

Jago nodded. 'I can accept that. But how did

Marshalls come into it?'

Henry stared at the carpet. 'I needed money,' he said with difficulty. 'Oh, I had a good income, but we lived up to it. I suppose everyone does nowadays. I had to settle the overdraft, and then I was told about this private clinic where they were getting wonderful results, not just curing the addiction, but rehabilitating the users afterwards. Only it wasn't cheap. And the most important thing was for Shelagh not to know. She was so proud of the children—we've never had any real problems with either of them before—and so happy too. I couldn't bear to see that end. I could have got a bank loan to pay the clinic fees, but I knew she'd see it on our statements. I didn't know where to turn. And then, one evening, I got a phone call.'

'From Paul Hollings?' Jago asked.

Henry nodded jerkily. 'I'd never met him before, but he seemed to know a lot about me—as if he'd been having me watched. He said he understood I was having some family troubles, and that he'd like to help. I told him to go to hell, but he called again, and eventually I arranged to meet him.' He laughed, the sound bitter. 'Oh, he made it sound so easy at first. All he wanted, he said, was "a friend at court"—someone to plead Marshalls' case for a takeover with the board. For that, he said, he'd be willing to pay a retainer. And that's all it was, at first. It was only later that he started asking about tenders, getting me to pass on the figures we were submitting so that they could underbid us.'

'As you did today?' said Jago.

He nodded. 'He was really putting the pressure on about Craigmore. He said it was make or break time. I told him you'd installed the safe, but he wouldn't listen. Then, when I saw Ashley had got hold of the file somehow, I phoned Hollings and he invited her out to lunch, to make sure she'd be out of the office for a while.'

'There was no need to go to those lengths,' Jago said harshly. 'I'd left the bloody file on my desk, waiting for you. I'd even given you an excuse to come to the office. You see, I too did not wish my wife to be involved. You'd already used her, and her friendship for you, too often as it was.'

'Or not enough,' Ashley put in softly. 'Henry, if you needed money, why didn't you come to me? I'd have been glad to help.'

His face was wretched. 'Because I couldn't guarantee that Shelagh wouldn't find out somehow through you. Ashley, the last thing I wanted was to hurt you, believe me. But the Marshalls takeover was beginning to seem so inevitable ...'

'In that case, why did you warn me about it— bring me back from abroad?'

'He had to,' Jago told her. 'Because people were beginning to notice his lack of action, and comment on it. As it was, he left it as long as possible, thinking it would be impossible for you to reverse the way things were going. When you came back, the takeover was as near a *fait accompli* as he could manage. The fact that I was back in town was inconvenient, but he counted on the rift between us being permanent. The news that we were getting married must have been like a thunderbolt.'

Henry winced. 'It was. And Hollings was wild with fury, I can tell you! But he said if you'd split up once, there was a chance it could happen again, and he'd work on that angle. And then he started talking about Craigmore. I told him things were different, that I thought you suspected something, but he wouldn't listen.'

'How very unwise,' Jago drawled silkily. 'Yes, I guessed there had to be a rotten apple in the barrel from that first board meeting. Clive Farnsworth had come to the same conclusion, and we had a very interesting private chat when the meeting was over. We decided the best thing was to supply you with the rope and let you hang yourself. At the same time, knowing how fond Ashley was of you, I wanted to keep her out of it. She'd have had to know eventually, of course, so I tried to prepare her a little—drop a few hints, to cushion the blow when it came.' He shook his head. 'But you had me worried, Henry. I thought you'd seen the trap I'd set for you and sidestepped it. But then when Katie told me you'd been in Ashley's office while she was at lunch, I breathed again.' He shrugged. 'I don't know what figure Marshalls are putting on the Craigmore tender, but this time we'll give them a run for their money.'

Shelagh's voice shook. 'And all to protect me. Oh God, Henry, how could you?'

He turned on her almost fiercely. 'Because I thought you'd blame yourself, think you'd been deficient in some way. And you haven't. You've been a wonderful mother—the best wife a man could want. I wanted to preserve everything we had together, keep it intact for you. I'd have done anything—anything ...'

She took his hand and held it.

Jago got to his feet. 'I don't think there's anything more to be said. It's time we were going.'

Henry looked up at him. 'What's going to happen?'

Jago's brows rose. 'I think—discreet early retirement on full pension, don't you? Don't come in to clear your desk. I'll have your things sent to you.'

He paused. 'Of course, any future arrangements you come to with Marshalls will be your own business, naturally.'

Henry said heavily, 'There won't be any. You've been—generous. I don't deserve that.'

'No.' Jago's mouth twisted. 'But I presume that's what my wife would want me to do—for the sake of past friendship.'

Henry looked at her. 'Ashley, my dear, I'm sorry.'

'So am I,' she said quietly. 'More sorry than you'll ever know.'

In the car, silence enfolded them both like a web. Ashley said at last, 'That was—awful.'

'Yes, it was,' Jago agreed. 'I'd planned to handle the whole thing at the office, after I'd altered our tender, and then break the news to you at home. But when I sent for Henry, his secretary said he'd already left.'

'Couldn't it have waited—until Monday?'

'Perhaps,' Jago said abruptly. 'But I don't want him back in the building. He's done enough damage.'

'I suppose so.' She moistened her lips with the tip of her tongue. 'And I never saw it coming—not even when you made me take another look at those other tenders. I never thought of him.'

'Why should you?' he asked flatly. 'Henry was someone you trusted implicitly, and anyway couldn't prove a thing. I had to make him give himself away—rely on the fact that he was getting jumpier by the day.'

She said, 'Poor Shelagh ...'

'She's a tough lady,' said Jago. 'She'll pull something together out of this mess. Henry shoul have recognised this, and shared his problems with her, instead of assuming that because he'd gone to pieces, she would too.'

'You're hard on him ...'

'He was hard on us.' His face was set, implacable. 'For God's sake, you little fool, he almost lost you Landons. Don't you realise that?'

'Yes,' she admitted in a subdued voice.

He shot her an edged look. He said, 'About Hollings. I hope it hasn't hurt you to realise his attentions had an ulterior motive?'

'He never fooled me for a moment,' Ashley said quietly.

'I'm pleased to hear it,' he said. 'Poor Ash, you haven't had a great deal of luck with the men in your life. A fiancé who couldn't remain faithful for the duration of your engagement, a father who wanted to sacrifice you to his own commercial ambitions, and an old friend who sold you out.' He paused. 'I thought you found Paul Hollings attractive.'

Ashley shrugged. 'In an obvious way, I suppose he is. But I'm not as naïve as I once was.'

He turned the car into the drive. 'I suppose I should be glad to hear you say so, but oddly I'm not. Although I suppose it will make it easier to leave you to your own devices.'

'What do you mean?' She followed him into the house, the sudden thudding of her heart sounding an alarm call.

'I've had an offer to go back to the States,' he said curtly. He walked into the drawing room, clicking on the light, and busied himself pouring two brandies from the decanter on a side table.

Ashley dropped her wrap on the sofa. Dry-mouthed, she asked, 'Are you going to take—this offer?'

'I have no reason not to, although I wouldn't leave until Landons has turned the corner, if that's what you're worried about.' Jago lifted his glass in a mock toast. 'I won't renege on my business obligations to you, Ashley. As for the personal ones—don't pretend you wouldn't find it a relief to rid of me. You've learned to accept my presence in your bed, but you don't welcome it.'

'I see,' she said numbly. 'So what will happen—about this house, for instance?'

'You can stay here. And if the thought of having to share it with Erica concerns you, then forget it She won't be coming back here.'

'She'll be going to the States with you?' Ashley took a gulp of brandy.

'Good God, no,' Jago said flatly. 'I'd as soon take a black mamba.'

'But she said ...'

He put his glass down and came over to her. His mouth was set. 'Listen,' he said. 'I am not responsible for Erica's fantasies. I never have been nor do I plan to be. In fact one of my priorities apart from dealing with Henry Brett, has been to get her out of my hair once and for all. And today did it. I got her to sell me her life interest in the estate. The negotiations have been a nightmare She's been blowing hot and cold, wringing every ounce of drama out of the situation, looking for an excuse to give me hassle, and jack the price up—yet again,' he added grimly. He sent her a wry look. 'That's why I couldn't let you summarily dismiss that ghoul of a housekeeper. If Erica had found out, she'd probably have thrown a tantrum and backed out of the deal. But now you can fire the woman with my blessing.'

'But you were always with her. You were drinking champagne, and you didn't come back to the office ...' Ashley's voice was trembling.

'I felt the situation deserved champagne, but that's as far as the celebration went. The rest of the afternoon we spent at the lawyers, signing the necessary papers.'

She said, 'Why didn't you tell me?'

Jago sighed. 'Because I didn't want to build up your hopes too soon. She was threatening to change her mind right up to the last moment, but fortunately she's even more mercenary than she is spiteful, and I was able to make her an offer, finally, that she couldn't refuse.'

'I thought you were in love with her,' Ashley whispered.

'You must be confusing me with my cousin Giles,' he said courteously. 'Now he, poor devil, was crazy about her, so much so that he never even thought of giving her the hiding she so richly deserves.'

'But she told me,' Ashley said blankly. 'She let me think ...'

'I'm sure she did, and revelled in every minute of it,' he said unsmilingly. 'But I'm telling you here and now that I have never for even a fleeting moment cherished any warm thoughts for Erica. I was sorry for her, initially, when Giles died, because I thought it had hit her harder than she expected.' His mouth curled. 'But I soon changed my mind. Her plan is now to be a merry widow in St Tropez, or Marbella, and bloody good luck to her.'

He paused, his hazel eyes ironic as they rested on her. 'No, my sweet wife, I, for my sins, have always been in love with you, almost from the first damnable moment I set eyes on you. And I wanted to marry you more than I've ever wanted anything

in my life, although I admit I suffered a slight check
when I discovered you were only marrying me from
a sense of duty, to provide Silas with the successor
he wanted for Landons.'

She said hoarsely, 'But that's what you wanted—
not me, but Landons ...'

'Don't be insane,' he said coldly. 'I hadn't the
slightest interest in Landons, nor did I want to be
groomed for future stardom on the board, as Silas
suggested. I'd already made up my mind to take
that American job, but when I told him so he let
me know, regretfully but very plainly, that I couldn't
expect you to go with me. Why would you go to
America, he asked me, when you were only
marrying me to ensure the future wellbeing of the
company?' He gave a bitter laugh. 'A lot of things
became clear at that moment. I realised, for
instance, why you froze me off every time I tried to
get near you. When I mentioned this to Silas, he
got very embarrassed, and said he'd talk to you—
make sure you knew your duty when the time
came. His very words,' he added flatly.

'Silas—said that?' Ashley's head was spinning
crazily. 'But he wouldn't—he couldn't ...'

'Oh, but he did,' Jago corrected. He shook his
head. 'I didn't want to believe it either. You see
I'd kept telling myself that somewhere underneath
that almost hysterical frigidity there was a warm
loving girl, and that if I was patient enough, I'd find
her. Silas' revelations gave me a whole new insight
into our relationship—one that, frankly, made me
sick to my stomach. I felt as if I'd been poleaxed.
After I left Silas, I went into town, with the
intention of getting roaring, stinking drunk.' He
finished his brandy and set down the glass. 'The
rest, of course, you remember, far more lucidly

than I do.'

'That—girl ...'

He nodded. 'Exactly. I have to confess that between leaving the bar and waking to find myself in bed with a complete stranger, and you battering the door down, there's nothing but a total blur.' He shrugged. 'Not that it excuses anything, of course, but I gather from my companion's hostile remarks before she left that I'd passed out before fulfilling any of her expectations. So I was technically faithful to you all along.' His smile was self-derisive.

Ashley swallowed. 'That—night, I'd seen Erica. She told me you were only marrying me for the company, and that I should allow you some freedom before tying you down. Finding you with that girl just seemed to—confirm everything she'd said.'

There was a silence. Then Jago said quietly, 'So that's what it was. I'd wondered, naturally, how you just happened to—turn up at the flat like that. Not that it matters now.'

'Why doesn't it matter?' she asked tensely.

He shrugged. 'Because it's time we cut our losses, Ashley. I should have never have pushed you into this marriage. It's been a disaster from first to last, and I have no right to keep you tied to me, no matter what I may have said. But when I walked back into your life, and saw you looking so anxious, so burdened, all I could think of was taking it all off your shoulders.' He sighed. 'I thought, in my arrogance, you see, that if I loved you enough, you'd be bound to care for me in return. How wrong I was!' His voice held a kind of weary finality. 'But you don't have to worry any more. I won't inflict my presence on you for much longer. I'll wait to make sure we have the Craigmore project in the bag before I leave for the States, but now that you haven't Henry to contend with, you should find things much easier. I could remain nominally chairman of the board, if they'd prefer, but you'll have your company back again, Ashley.' He smiled faintly. 'And, more importantly, your life.'

Ashley felt as if she'd been turned to stone. She fought for words, but none would come. Seeing him turn away and walk towards the door was the spur she needed. She flew after him.

'Jago.' It was barely more than a croak. He swung round, the brooding hazel eyes assessing her pallor, the sharp glitter of tears on her face. She flung herself at him, clinging frantically to his shoulders, pressing little heated kisses on his face and throat, her voice feverishly whispering, 'Don' leave me ...' over and over again.

His hands closed on her, not gently, pushing her backwards so that he could look into her eyes. His face was incredulous, but underneath there was a dawning hope.

He said hoarsely, 'You—want me?'

'I love you. You can't leave me! You have to take me with you!' She beat on her chest with clenched fists. 'Wherever you go, I want to be with you.'

He said, 'You will be,' and it was somehow more than a marriage vow.

He picked her up in his arms and carried her to the sofa. He sat cradling her on his lap, his arm wrapped round her, kissing the tears from her face murmuring to her until she was calm again. The they were very still together, Ashley's face buried in the curve of his throat, his lips against her hair closer in some strange way than they had ever been, even at moments of greatest intimacy.

At last he sighed a little, and cupped her chin in his fingers, making her face him.

'Three wasted years,' he said huskily. 'Darling, why didn't you tell me—why didn't you let me know? You were always so cold ...'

'I was frightened,' she confessed.

Jago looked remorseful. 'Of something I did? God, sweetheart ...'

'No.' Ashley stroked his face with her fingertips. 'Of myself. I—I didn't know what was happening to me. Every time you touched me, I seemed to—go up in flames, and I was overwhelmed.' She flushed. 'You see, all Silas had ever said was that no matter what the permissive society had to say, men still valued purity in the women they were going to marry. He gave me the impression that sex was something a decent woman—just put up with. I couldn't tell him that when I was with you I felt neither pure nor decent. I was terrified in case I was unnatural in some way, and there was no one I could talk to about it.'

'You could have talked to me,' Jago told her gently. 'I was going to be your husband.'

Ashley sighed. 'I suppose I was a little in awe of you,' she said slowly. 'Marrying you was like having every dream come true at once. I kept telling myself that once we really were married, everything would be all right. That you'd make everything all right.'

He groaned. 'I wish I'd shared your certainty,' he said ruefully. 'At first, I told myself you were just shy, but that you'd relax when you came to trust me. Only you never did. The wedding was coming nearer and nearer, and you still shrank every time I tried to touch you.' He shook his head. 'My conversation with Silas was the last straw. Being saddled with a duty wife was a terrifying prospect.'

'How could he have said such a thing?' Ashley asked helplessly.

Jago shrugged. 'Because he believed it. He was a good business man, darling, but his knowledge of human nature left a lot to be desired. He should have seen that Henry was a potential weak link in his chain, long before you took over. Silas was obsessed by Landons, and he assumed everyone else had to be too, including you. Our marriage fitted his plans, and the fact that our own plans might be different would never have occured to him. He was genuinely shocked when I told him I was going to the States and taking you with me. I think he honestly thought that you'd share his viewpoint.'

'He'd never discussed why I was marrying you,' she said slowly. 'He was delighted about it. I thought it was for my sake, at first anyway. Then I began to wonder—odd things he said about you being "a chip off the old block", as if he was congratulating himself on having—engineered the whole thing. I—I began to ask myself questions. For instance, why had you talked about making me happy, but said nothing about being in love with me?'

There was a silence, then Jago said quietly, 'My God.' His arms gathered her closer still. 'I was trying hard not to frighten you, sweetheart. I thought if I started telling you even half the things I felt for you and about you, I might panic you into a complete retreat. You have a lot to forgive me for.'

'No,' she began to protest, but he laid a silencing, caressing finger on her lips.

'I should have taken longer over wooing,' he said softly. 'I should have made absolutely certain that you knew I loved you and wanted you for yourself

I should have come to you that night and demanded an explanation, instead of heading for the nearest damned bar.'

'I don't blame you for that,' she told him, her mouth trembling into an unsteady smile. 'I was shattered too, after speaking to Erica. I wish I'd made for the same bar.'

'Erica and Silas.' He groaned. 'They couldn't have done a better number on us if they'd been in collusion! I should have realised that bitch would get at you if she could, and protected you better. That's the main reason I was so keen to buy her off this time round. In case she started sharpening her claws on you. It never occured to me that she might have already begun.'

She said, 'Jago, why didn't you come after me—that night?'

'I did. But by the time I'd dragged on some clothes, got rid of my visitor, and pulled myself together, you were nowhere to be found. And first thing in the morning, I got my ring back, and a message making it clear you didn't want to see me again. It seemed you couldn't wait to be rid of me. I decided Silas had been quite right, and you had only been marrying me for the company's sake, after all. That you were glad to have an excuse to call the whole thing off. So I told myself I was better off without you, and cleared out to the States.' He smiled crookedly. 'But try as I might—and I did try, darling—I couldn't forget you. Any fragment of news about you that came my way, I used to treasure obsessively. Giles used to tell me how you were getting on. He was always very fond of you. And then he died, and I had to come back, only to find the town and the newspapers full of rumours about Landons and its problems.' He grimaced. 'It seemed like a way to get back to you again, although I told myself I was simply curious to see if you were prepared to sell yourself a second time. But it made no difference. After seeing you at the Country Club that night, I was lost. I had to have you,' his voice grew almost sombre, 'by any means available. You looked so beautiful, so sure of yourself, I told myself you couldn't possibly still be the same innocent virgin I'd loved and lost. Witham was lucky I didn't kill him,' he added savagely.

Ashley choked back a giggle. 'Poor Martin!'

'To hell with him.' Jago tugged gently at the lobe of her ear with his teeth. 'Save your compassion for me.'

She smiled into his eyes. 'Oh, I had a different sort of comfort in mind.' She moved against him with a deliberate and delicate sensuality, hearing the breath catch in his throat.

He said unevenly, 'Tell me more—or even better still, show me.'

She kissed him slowly, running her tongue along the curve of his lower lip, feeling his muscles stir and clench under the first tentative exploration of her hands.

She was his love, and the realisation made the blood sing for joy in her veins, but tonight he wanted her to be his lover, and it would be her pleasure to please him, to return some of the delight he had taught her. To let him know beyond question that she belonged to him completely, to give him the reassurance he seemed to need.

Tonight, she thought, their marriage would begin. And her heart soared.

Harlequin Presents

Coming Next Month

Available in October wherever paperback books are sold, or through Harlequin Reader Service:

In the U.S.
901 Fuhrmann Blvd.
P.O. Box 1397
Buffalo, N.Y. 14240-1397

In Canada
P.O. Box 603
Fort Erie, Ontario
L2A 5X3

Take 4 books & a surprise gift FREE

SPECIAL LIMITED-TIME OFFER

Mail to **Harlequin Reader Service**®

In the U.S.
901 Fuhrmann Blvd.
P.O. Box 1394
Buffalo, N.Y. 14240-1394

In Canada
P.O. Box 609
Fort Erie, Ontario
L2A 5X3

YES! Please send me 4 free Harlequin Romance® novels and my free surprise gift. Then send me 8 brand-new novels every month as they come off the presses. Bill me at the low price of $1.99 each*—an 11% saving off the retail price. There are no shipping, handling or other hidden costs. There is no minimum number of books I must purchase. I can always return a shipment and cancel at any time. Even if I never buy another book from Harlequin, the 4 free novels and the surprise gift are mine to keep forever.   118 BPR BP7F

*Plus 89¢ postage and handling per shipment in Canada.

Name	(PLEASE PRINT)	
Address		Apt. No.
City	State/Prov.	Zip/Postal Code

This offer is limited to one order per household and not valid to present subscribers. Price is subject to change.   DOR-SUB-1D